the issue with bad boy roommates

PIPER RAYNE

Cover Design: By Hang Le

1st Line Editor: Joy Editing

2nd Line Editor: My Brother's Editor

Proofreader: My Brother's Editor

I was only looking for a roommate...

I'm the town widow.

Not the only one, but the youngest by far.

My husband died one year after our wedding, casting me as the charity case in my small Alaskan town.

Since then, everyone—including my big family—try to keep me busy as if that will stop the haunting memories from resurfacing.

Do I know it's time to move on? Of course, but that's easier said than done.

Then Van Adler rides into town. His bad boy vibe complete with his motorcycle and tattoos causes my body to fill with need for the first time since my husband's death.

To make matters worse, he's the one who answered my ad for a roommate. Sharing the close quarters of our two-bedroom apartment means I have to set some ground rules like keeping his rippled abs covered. Soon we become friends, he's making me dinners, and we're binge-watching television shows all night.

The more our lives intertwine, the more I start to fall for him. Leaving me wondering, can you find the love of your life twice in one lifetime?

THE
ISSUE
WITH
BAD BOY
ROOMMATES

one

"No one has answered my ad for a roommate." I push my laptop away from me after checking my email, and the saltshaker falls over.

Lance picks it up and shakes it over his left shoulder. "Left, right?" he asks our other cousin, Easton, who's busy beside me on what I can see is another dating app.

"Nothing is gonna happen if you don't throw salt over your shoulder." Easton shakes his head but doesn't look up.

"I think you're the one who spilled it, Brin, so you should sprinkle it over your shoulder too." Lance holds the saltshaker in front of me from across the table.

"A sprinkle of salt isn't going to ward off anything bad happening to me. The dark cloud over my head for the past four years is proof of that." I take the saltshaker and place it on the table.

"You're tempting fate." Lance straightens his tie and throws it over his shoulder when our waitress slides his tomato soup and salad in front of him. He almost always gets the same thing when we come to Lard Have Mercy.

I pick up the saltshaker and toss salt over my left

shoulder to stop this ridiculous conversation and get back to the immediate problem I need to solve—finding a roommate.

"I don't get it. You knew Calista was gonna move out." Easton finally pockets his phone when his double-decker BLT slides in front of him.

Calista is our oldest cousin and was my roommate, but last year, she married the love of her life—a professional soccer player. Although she's been living in Chicago, she's been nice enough to pay the rent. But she's returning to our small Alaskan town for the off-season this week, and they've found a house, which means I need to find another roommate.

"Hence the ad," I deadpan.

"Maybe we should tweak it. It was a little..." Lance isn't going to tell me what specifically is wrong, he's too nice. Instead, he glances at Easton, who's always happy to give his honest opinion, even when you don't want it.

"Anal retentive," Easton says. "Cold. It reads like you'll have a chore chart on the fridge, and there will be consequences if you don't get a gold star next to your name."

I huff. "It was not that bad. I'm not ending up with some slob."

Easton busies himself with taking the tomatoes out of his BLT.

"Why don't you just tell them you don't want tomatoes?" Lance asks but gets no answer.

"Don't you ever look at your life and think... how did I get here?" I put my laptop in my messenger bag tucked between the wall and me.

They shovel food in their mouths so they don't have to answer.

"My mom and dad want to help me with the rent or have me stay with them." I roll my eyes.

Lance shakes his head, grabs his soda, and sucks down a third of his Coke before wiping his mouth. "That's the worst thing you could do. I'm proud of you, Brin. You're living on your own and learning to run Bailey Timber. Soon things will fall in place." He notices I've yet to get a plate of food and points at the empty spot in front of me. "Where's your food?"

"Hasn't come yet." I look to find the waitress, but Easton catches her attention first and she practically runs over. Of course she does.

"Hey, Mindy, my cousin here hasn't gotten her food?"

She looks at my empty spot.

"The chopped salad?" I gently remind her.

Her eyes widen and she nods. "I'll be right back."

"Thanks, Mindy," Easton says and winks.

I groan.

"Please tell me you haven't scored with the waitress?" Lance says to Easton.

"No way, she's jailbait." He picks up half his sandwich and holds it out to me. "Have some of mine while you're waiting."

"No thanks." I shake my head and blow out a breath. "I'm not really hungry anyway."

He takes a bite and concentrates on his meal. They both do, and for the millionth time in my life, I wish one of them would've been born a girl. But no, I'm stuck being the only girl. All three of us were born within hours of one another, and we've been pegged with the nickname the Bailey Triplets our whole lives, after our family name. Even if Lance's and my last name isn't Bailey since it's our moms' maiden name.

Easton pinches my arm like our great-grandma Dori used to do.

"What the hell?" I glare at him.

"You're too thin. You look better when your face is fuller," he says.

I turn in the booth and stare at him. It takes him three bites before he looks at Lance and then at me. Easton's brown hair, with hints of auburn he inherited from his mom, is perfectly styled into a messy look, and it's almost aggravating how it always looks so perfectly unkempt. He smiles and slides his tongue out to lick the mayo from the corner of his mouth.

With as much frost as I can put in my voice, I say, "Thanks for the advice. Should I trade in my chopped salad for a burger and fries?"

"I would," he mumbles around his mouthful of food.

"Don't listen to him." Lance pushes his plate to the edge of the table, wipes his mouth with his paper napkin, and puts it on the plate. "You're beautiful as always. I hate to cut this short, but I have to fly to New York this afternoon for a few days."

"Lance, you didn't even help me with the roommate ad."

He straightens his tie down his shirt and slides out of the booth to put on the suit jacket he left hanging on the coat tree. "I'll write something and email it to you on the plane."

"Daddy's plane… must be nice." Easton pokes fun at the fact that Lance's dad comes from an uber-wealthy Manhattan family that owns a chain of hotels. "Why don't you just live in New York? You spend enough time there."

"Do you have opinions on all of our lives?" I ask him.

He shrugs. "Suggestions. Mere suggestions."

"Well, I have a few for you. The first is that you're going to get someone pregnant or catch an STI if you don't stop with those apps." I look pointedly at the phone in his pocket.

He drops his sandwich and narrows his eyes at me. "I don't think you'd like it if I slut-shamed you, so don't do it to me."

I look at Lance, who's busy straightening his messenger bag. How on earth did my best friend, Kenzie, ever become torn between these two? They couldn't be more opposite. "A little help here?"

Lance glances between the two of us. "Easton has a point. It's his life, his dick. It wouldn't be a bad idea for you to get some too."

I laugh. He's crazy if he thinks I'd actually mess around with someone.

Lance stands to his full height, gives Easton a fist bump, and me a smile since I'm locked in the booth by Easton. "I'll shoot you an email."

He turns to leave, but he runs into a guy who's just come into Lard Have Mercy.

"Excuse me," the guy says.

He and Lance do a sidestep dance until they both stop. Lance laughs and the guy glances my way before nodding and heading to the back hallway toward the bathrooms.

After he's gone, Lance looks at us. "Who's that?"

I shrug. "How would I know?"

"Whoever he is, he's huge. Not someone I'd wanna mess with." Easton pushes his plate away and gulps down his water.

"Here you go." Mindy puts a Caesar salad in front of me before walking away.

My cousins stare at me.

"This is my life." I pick up my fork and stab at the lettuce because I don't have time for them to prepare another one.

"See you two." Lance waves and leaves, looking like the Wall Street guy he isn't. But he doesn't completely fit in in our small town either, because he spends so much time in New York. I have my suspicions as to why he doesn't just move there, but I've never outright asked.

We say bye and I hip-check Easton, almost making him fall out of the booth. "What the—"

"Go to the other side now that Lance is gone." I nod toward the empty side of the booth.

"Normal people just ask," he says, sliding around to the other side.

I situate myself in the middle of the bench seat and start back in on my salad.

Meanwhile, the guy who almost ran into Lance comes out of the bathroom and sits at the table by the window. He plops down a duffel bag on the chair across from him and takes out the local paper.

"What are we looking at?" Easton whispers from across the table.

"Nothing."

He glances over his shoulder, and I throw a crouton at him. "Don't."

He picks it up from his shirt and pops it into his mouth, chomping down dramatically and loudly. I narrow my eyes at him.

He shrugs after getting a good look at the guy. "I bet he's here for your dad. Look at his tats."

I saw his tattoos and how they go all the way up his arms. I also notice the bulging biceps, the dark hair styled short, the vibrant blue eyes. He's definitely attractive. You'd have to be blind not to notice.

"You like him," Easton says.

"Um. I don't know him. How could I like him?" I fork my salad, keeping my eyes down.

"Look at your cheeks. You're blushing."

I glance up at Easton through my eyelashes. "Stop it."

"It'd be good for you. I know you think I'm some manwhore, but come on, Brin, it's been years since Sawyer died and I know you haven't gotten any. Maybe sex would make that dark cloud over your head disappear."

Hearing Sawyer's name feels like a blow to the chest. It's been three and a half years, so it doesn't happen a lot anymore, but it still catches me off guard.

"Having sex is not going to make the cloud disappear." I shake my head.

"Judge all you want, but I live a happy life." He shrugs.

"I don't remember it being under my control that I became a widow as a newlywed."

Sawyer's death set off a chain of events that led me to where I am today. After he died, I had to sell the house we'd paid too much for, so I ended up in the hole. Once I made good on that, I didn't have any money left and had to move in with Calista, who's now married and left me to cover the rent myself. Needless to say, this is not where I expected to end up after I said "I do" at twenty years old.

Easton leans back in the booth, one arm stretched out, the other on the table and fiddling with his water, his gaze on me. "Eventually you need to pick yourself up out of this funk. We've all tried to help, and we've all failed. I know it sucks having your husband die shortly after you got married. You think because I don't want a commitment in my life right now that I don't understand how awful it is?"

I drop my fork in my salad and it's so loud that I swear the entire restaurant stares at me, including that guy by the window. Our eyes briefly connect, and he lifts his lips in a welcoming smile, but I turn away before it can affect me.

"It's my life. You can imagine, but you don't live it. And I'm not going to sleep my way through our small town with the hopes that one day Sawyer will be erased from my memory."

How did our conversation turn to Sawyer once again? We're supposed to be talking about the roommate ad and how I've had no responses.

He holds up his hands. "Truce, okay?"

I nod, exasperated. "Okay."

He pulls out his wallet, so I guess he's about to leave too. "I just miss you. I miss the old Brinley who enjoyed life. I feel like, after the accident, you just stopped living." He slides out of the booth and drops some bills on the table. "I have to go. My dad wants me to talk to a few of his players. I'll call you later."

My uncle Austin is the high school baseball coach, and since Easton is a professional baseball player, he'll often chat with the team during his off-season.

"Okay."

He kisses my forehead. "Sorry," he says because he never wants to leave anything unfinished.

I shake my head. "It's okay. I know I have to move on."

And that's the truth. I do know I can't mourn Sawyer forever, and I need to move on with my life, but that's a scary prospect to think of, let alone actually do it.

"Maybe you need more time." I shake my head and he chuckles.

"Now you want to say the right thing."

"I'm an asshole. What can I say? I'm not good at sugar-coating."

"Bye, Easton," I say and push him away.

"Love you!" he screams as he leaves the restaurant.

The sound makes tat boy glance up from the paper he's reading. When he sees Easton, he buries his head in the paper again.

I finish my salad and I'm about to pull out my money when I see Easton left enough for the entire bill.

"Excuse me?"

I peer up toward the deep voice at the end of the table. The deep voice is attached to the tatted-up guy, and I realize that the distance did not do him justice. My heart beats and my stomach somersaults. Holy shit, he's so good-looking, he has to be a model.

"Hi?" I say way too mouselike. My mom would lecture me about it if she heard it.

"Could you point me in the direction of Lucky's? I have to see a guy about a job." He smiles, and it kind of feels like being in a tractor beam—I can't look away.

"Um…"

Easton's words ring in my head. Maybe I need to jump back into something. This guy is definitely not someone I'd ever fall for—he's a stranger in town. Who knows how long he'll stick around.

"How about I show you?"

VAN

The blonde slides out of the booth and stands to her full height, which only comes up to my chin, but I like that. She meticulously puts on her coat, buttoning it, then positioning her computer bag on her shoulder to lie crosswise over her chest. If not for the jacket, the strap would've slid between her tits, and I'd be a liar if I said I wouldn't have liked that view.

"All done?" Mindy comes over and picks up the money her boyfriend must've tossed on the table.

"Yes, thank you." She smiles at the girl, but the waitress's eyes are on me as if I'm an all-you-can-eat sundae bar.

I motion with my hand for the blonde to lead the way, and I walk behind her toward the exit. Every set of eyes in the place watches us leave. I'm well aware of how fast rumors fly around a small town, and I have to think we might just be the next one based on all the attention we're garnering.

We exit the diner and I notice the way she runs her thumb over the bare ring finger of her left hand a bunch of times. She opens her mouth to speak, but I interrupt her before she can just give me directions and leave.

"Thanks a lot for doing this." I pull her back into our bubble because there's something here. Yeah, I'm attracted to her—who wouldn't be? Gorgeous set of tits on a thin frame with an ass made to grab. And I do love blondes. But before I instigate anything, I need to know how serious it is with the boyfriend. Maybe he's just some guy she's seeing, but they haven't decided to be exclusive yet.

"Sure." She walks down the sidewalk and I keep pace with her.

People smile and wave. Some say hello as we pass by, but none of them stop to talk to her. Maybe because she's with me. They all look confused, and I can understand why. The two of us probably don't look all that compatible, her with her buttoned-up professional look and me with my jeans and leather jacket.

When I decided to spend my eight-week leave from the Coast Guard here in Lake Starlight, I knew that as an outsider, I'd have to answer questions about myself, but I learned how to be vague a long time ago.

"I'm assuming you're a lifer?" I ask, straightening my duffel bag on my shoulder.

"Lifer?"

"Everyone we pass seems to know you."

"Oh... yeah. I've lived here my entire life and both my parents did before me, so..." It sounds like there's so much more she could tell me, but she doesn't.

"Then I guess I asked the right woman for directions."
She smiles.

Maybe I misinterpreted her glances my way at the diner. Maybe she doesn't want anything to do with me other than to show me to Lucky's. Lucky's isn't that far, so once we reach it, we stop and she signals to the doors.

I take in the place. "I thought it would be bigger."

"There aren't a lot of big things in this town." Her eyes trace over my body and I like them on me. It's been a long time since I've gotten this much interest from a woman I just met.

"I'm starting to see that." I bite the inside of my cheek. "I hope your boyfriend doesn't get upset that you showed me how to get here?"

"Boyfriend?" Her head tilts to the side.

"The guy at the diner? The one who said he loved you when he left."

She laughs and stops when she sees my confusion. "That's my cousin, and he definitely isn't boyfriend material for anyone."

I rock back on my heels. If I didn't have an interview, I'd try to spend time with her. "Can I get your number then? Maybe you could show me around while I'm here."

The innuendo is obvious in my tone, and her eyes widen for a moment as though she's surprised I'm asking. There's no way this woman doesn't get hit on every damn day.

"How long are you here for?" she asks.

If my commander at the Coast Guard has anything to say about it, it'll be eight weeks. But I don't say that. "I'm not sure. I'm not on a time clock."

She smiles and nods. "Um... sure."

I put my password in my phone, go to my contacts, and hand it to her. Her hands tremble a bit as she holds it, her thumbs resting over the screen as if she's second-guessing giving me her information. She looks at me before typing anything, and I smile at her. Something is stopping her from giving me her number.

A man comes out of the tattoo parlor next door. I noticed Smokin' Guns when I came into town and was thinking maybe I'd add to my collection while I'm here. He doesn't bother looking at me, but he stares at the back of the blonde, clearing his throat loudly enough that he's easily heard.

Her alarmed eyes lift to mine, and she hands me back my phone. Glancing over her shoulder, her hands shake more, so she clenches them at her sides. "Sorry, I should go. I'm sure I'll see you around, not many places to hide."

I nod, a little disappointed. "Thanks."

She hurries over to the man who's definitely older than her.

"Hey," she says when she reaches him and walks into the shop.

The man's eyes finally meet mine, and he studies me for a second. "Hey, Brinley."

He gives me what I interpret as a warning glare. Then he steps inside, and the door shuts after him.

I shake my head, opening the door to Lucky's. This isn't exactly what I thought my first day here would be like. Inside, I find a small bar with booths by the window and tables of four placed where there's room. There are dart boards and pool tables in the back, along with a jukebox. Other than a group of four elderly people in a booth, the place is empty.

A guy comes out of the back as I step up to the bar and drop my duffel bag on the floor.

He smiles and crosses the room to me. "You must be Van." He puts his hand out in front of me.

"Nate?" My eyebrows rise.

"Yeah. Can I get you something?"

"A water?"

"Sure thing." He moves down the bar, grabs a bottle of water from the fridge, and calls to the booth with the elderly people, "Alice, do you need anything? Because I'm gonna be busy for twenty minutes or so."

A red-haired lady peeks out of the booth and shamelessly looks me up and down, her eyes widening when she reaches my eyes again. "Um... who is he?"

Nate shakes his head. "He's my interview."

She waves him off. "He's hired. You're going to get a lot more women in here with him behind the bar."

"And what does that say about me?" Nate looks offended.

"Stop looking for compliments," she says, then she turns her attention back to me. "Good luck. Not that you'd need it in my book."

I have no idea how to respond, so I just smile.

"Come on, Van, we'll talk over here." Nate nods to the farthest table from the overly friendly geriatric. Once we're both seated, he says, "I'm really sorry. They're from a retirement center in town and they hang out here sometimes while I'm getting ready for the evening shift. They act like they're in some secret club, but from what I overhear, all they talk about is the food at the home and who's sleeping with who."

I chuckle. "Good for them then."

He laughs. "That's what I said. When I get that old, I'm going there." He straightens the papers in his hands, and I catch he doesn't have a wedding ring. "So, you worked with Tony?"

I nod. "He's a great guy. Lucky bastard got transferred to Clearwater, Florida."

"And you're still up here in the frigid weather?"

I shrug. "I don't mind it up here."

"Yeah, Tony told me you're one of those guys—the more risk, the more adrenaline, the more you love it." He smirks. "So, you said you're on leave?"

"Yeah, eight weeks. Is that gonna be a problem?" I really wish I could be back with the Coast Guard right now, but my fucking commander ordered me to take time off. Since I can't sit around doing nothing for two months, I'm looking for something to occupy my time.

He laughs. "No problem at all. My right-hand guy just left and if I want to keep my relationship going with my girl, I cannot be here every night of the week."

"Then I'm your guy. While I'm here, I only plan on working. No need for any strings since I'll be gone soon."

He stares at me for a moment but doesn't say anything. His nonverbal cues tell me he's already typecast me as a one-night stand kinda guy. He's right to an extent. It's not that I never see a future with a wife or kids, but not while I'm in the prime of my life. I'm only twenty-six, and since you only get so many years to be a Coast Guard diver, I refuse to give it up for a regular piece of ass.

"You're hired." Nate nods.

"Thank you."

He pulls a few sheets of paper from a folder that is already at the table. "This is the wage plus your tips. We share when more than one bartender is on shift. Waitresses share with the bartenders and busboys. You find a place to stay in town yet?"

I pull out the newspaper. "I was just looking at apartment ads. There aren't many here, huh?"

"Unfortunately, the one drawback of Lake Starlight is the lack of rentals. There are some small houses for rent around the downtown area, but it'll be hard for you to find a short-term rental."

We continue talking about the area and he says that as long as I have transportation, I can check out the neighboring towns like Greywall or Winterberry Falls.

Alice surprises me by sitting next to me, taking the paper from my hands. "I thought I heard of someone I know who was putting an ad in the paper." She digs in her seashell purse and takes out a pair of reading glasses that are missing one arm. "Oh, here, you already have it circled." She hands the paper back to me.

I laugh because I circled that ad as a last-ditch effort. The person I'd be sharing space with doesn't sound very warm and cozy. "Oh, that one. I don't think I'd jive with that person."

Nate takes the paper from me and reads the ad, then shares a look with Alice.

"What's the look about?" I ask.

"Oh, nothing, you totally should call. I mean, this place." He points at another ad I had circled. "The guy is home all the time. One of those video gamers. And this one." He points at another one. "This ad is in the paper every other month because everyone they get moves out. I think the place is haunted or has mold or something."

He hands me the paper and I read the ad one more time.

ROOMMATE NEEDED TO SHARE A TWO-BEDROOM, *one-bathroom in Lake Starlight downtown area. Must be clean and organized. A list of chores will be assigned once you move in. Under no circumstances will I clean up after you. I'm neat and clean and expect my roommate to be as well. Guests are not welcome to stay and must be gone by ten o'clock. Must pay first and last month's rent plus security deposit. All necessary background checks will be required. No pets or felons allowed.*

"YEAH, I'm not sure. I mean, no guests and a chore list?"

Alice stands and stares down her nose at me. "Everyone sounds a little harsh in an ad. They don't want some hoarder moving in."

I tuck the paper in my bag because I'm still unsure, but I can't afford to keep staying at the Glacier Point Resort.

"Just call, sweetie. You're splitting the rent, so it is cheap."

Nate nods in agreement.

"Yeah, okay, I think I might."

After I've worked out the details of my employment with Nate, I leave and take a seat on a bench in the town square, then I call the number on the ad to say I'm interested in taking the room. Alice is right, it's only for a short time, and no one can really be as bad as this ad sounds.

three

I sit in my SUV outside the Anchorage airport, waiting for my cousin Calista and her new husband, Rylan, to arrive. Rylan is a professional soccer player, and they're returning to Lake Starlight for his off-season. Before I drop them at their place, we have to swing by my apartment, so they can pick up some stuff Calista left there.

In the end, I didn't have to change my ad because I got a response and the service that the paper uses did an entire background check on my behalf. So this evening, I'll have a new roommate.

I honk when I spot Calista and Rylan walking out of the sliding doors with their luggage. Calista waves and motions to Rylan, who has the brunt of the luggage weighing him down.

I get out of the SUV to help get everything in the back. "Hey, lovebirds."

I hug them and tell them about my new roommate while we figure out how to fit all their stuff in my vehicle. Eventually we manage to jigsaw all the luggage into the back of the SUV. Rylan climbs in the back, and Calista and I sit in the front.

"We'll swing by the apartment to grab your stuff before I drop you off. It's only, like, three boxes," I tell them, so they aren't surprised I'm not taking them to their new rental house that's big enough to fit half the Bailey clan.

"You could've dropped them at my mom's," Calista says, situating herself in the front seat while Rylan is ultra-relaxed in the back, arms spread out across the seat.

I wave her off. "It's fine. My roommate isn't going to be here for a little while anyway."

"How did you meet her?" Calista shifts in my direction.

"Through the paper." Calista opens her mouth to say something, but I add, "Now, before you argue, the newspaper has a background check service, and I did pay extra to look into her. No criminal record. Good credit report. Like, no debt. Not sure why she needs a roommate, to be honest."

"That's all good. I still don't like the idea of you living with a stranger." She glances at Rylan, who's on his phone in the back seat.

She's apologized to me so many times that Rylan doesn't want anyone living with them. I don't blame him in the slightest. I mean, they just got back together after years of weaving in and out of each other's lives. They're married and I know they want to start a family soon. The last thing they need is a bunch of Baileys hanging around. I remember the first months after Sawyer and I were married, and I want Calista to have that.

"I'm fine. I come from tough stock."

We laugh. It's true, my mom is a hard-ass, and my dad can definitely hold his own in a fight. Rumor has it that my dad protected Calista's dad more than once.

"What's her name?" Calista asks.

"Um... Carrie."

Finally, Calista stops asking questions and relaxes her head on the back of the seat. We get to Lake Starlight in no time, and I park along the curb in the downtown area outside our... er... my apartment.

"Did we miss anything?" Calista inspects the area, but not much changes around here.

"Nope. It's been quiet."

We all get out of the vehicle and head upstairs to the apartment. Rylan scopes out the apartment since he's never spent any time there, then he picks up the boxes.

As the sound of a motorcycle makes the windows shake, we all look at each other. It sounds as if it stops right in front of my building. A few seconds after the rumble of the engine cuts off, then the sound of footsteps on the stairs begins.

"Did someone new move in next door?" Calista asks.

I shake my head, not sure what that racket is all about.

Rylan walks over to the window and looks down at the street. "Smokin' Harley down there."

A knock sounds on the door and Calista answers as though it's still her place. My family is still so protective of me. A familiar-looking man wearing a T-shirt and jeans and tattoos all down his arms stands in the doorway, looking around the apartment as though he's wondering if he's in the right place.

Oh my god. It's him.

"Hey, I'm Carey." He holds out his hand to Calista. She glances at me for a second. "Are you Brinley?"

She shakes her head and points at me.

He smiles and holds out his hand to me as if we're strangers. Does he not remember we met only two days ago? If not for my dad pulling me away, I would have given him my number. "Nice to finally meet you."

"I thought it was Carrie with an *i-e*?" I say in a small voice.

"People get that wrong all the time. Ends in an *e-y* actually. Which room is mine?" He spots Rylan across the room and nods at him. "What's up, man? Carey."

He nods back. "Rylan."

"Point the way, and I'll be out of your hair," Carey says.

Are we really pretending?

"Um. Just around the corner to the right is your room."

He smiles and disappears down the hall.

I look at Calista with wide eyes.

"Nice guy. Let's go." Rylan comes to stand next to Calista.

Do I want them to leave? Especially when he doesn't remember me? I doubt this is a twin situation like with my uncles.

"You can't leave me here. She is a he!" I whisper-shout, admittedly panicking a bit. I figure there's safety in numbers.

"Actually, he's always been a he. Sounds like a mix-up with the paperwork," Calista says, and I stick my tongue out at her. "We can stay a little longer, right, babe?"

Rylan groans. "Fine." He drops the boxes and goes to sit on the couch.

"What do I do?" I bring my nails to my mouth.

We both look in the direction Carey went.

"I have no idea," she says.

Ten minutes later and the three of us are still sitting on the couch, pretending to watch television. Well, Rylan probably really is watching the sports channel, but I wait for Carey to walk out of his room.

I have so many questions. First, why did the agency not think it was important to mention that it was a male and not a female who answered the ad? I think most people would assume it was a female when they say the name Carrie. And second, why did he act as if we're strangers?

I'm not sure why, but I get up and take my wedding pictures out of the drawer I shoved them in and put them back on the shelves. I took them down to stop any questions from my new roommate, but tat boy, or Carey as I now know him, needs to know I'm not available like I suggested the other day.

"What are you doing?" Calista whispers.

"Just putting the pictures back up. I took them down, but…"

Calista stares at the bedroom door, which is shut. "And it's a good thing you packed them away."

I didn't pack them away, not really. I just hid them in drawers for the time being.

"I don't want him to get any ideas." I put out my favorite one of Sawyer and me by the lake on our wedding day. My gaze roams over my smile… I'm not sure I've shown that many teeth since that day.

"You're crazy." Calista picks them up one by one, shoves them back in the drawer, and shoves some other things on top of them. "This was a good thing you did. And a picture of a dead husband does not make you off-limits."

"Calista!"

She rests her hands on my upper arms. "What do you want to do? I'll have Rylan go in there and tell him there's been a mix-up and he can't stay here if you want."

"I'll what?" Rylan perks up on the couch. "Um… babe, did you see the size of that guy?" I'm not sure he's that concerned though, because he never tears his eyes away from the television.

"No, it's just…" I let my confession die on my lips. Do I want Calista to know that I've already met him? That I was going to take Easton's advice and maybe hook up with him because I thought he was a drifter and was going to be in and out of Lake Starlight, so no one would know I slept with him? But I'm too embarrassed to tell her, so even with her wide eyes, I shake my head. "It's my responsibility to tell him. In fact, you guys can go."

"Perfect." Rylan stands and grabs the boxes again.

"Ry!" Calista whisper-shouts.

"She said we could go." He nods at me.

I laugh because Rylan isn't a bad guy; he just wants to be alone with his new wife. If he felt I was in any real danger, he'd stick around, but I'm not nervous about Carey because I think he's dangerous.

"Really, go. I'll call you." I push Calista toward the door.

"But… Rylan." She glances at her husband.

"Haven't you ever seen *Single White Female*? Just because he's a guy doesn't mean he's dangerous. A girl could try to kill her too."

"Thanks for that." I cross my arms.

"I'm just saying I think you'll be fine." He shifts the boxes in his hands. "Let's just go take these over to Dion's and have him drive us home." He questions me with his eyes, asking if that's okay, and I nod.

Calista bites her lip and looks at me, then at the door. "I don't know. Maybe you should talk to him first, Ry."

He scoffs. "What am I going to say?"

Her arms flail. "I don't know. Like, don't mess with my cousin, she's delicate."

"Delicate?" I ask with exasperation. "No, you both need to go."

Calista gives Rylan a look and he groans, then puts down the boxes and stalks over to Carey's bedroom door.

"No!" I say a little too loudly.

Rylan knocks and he must be told to come in because he walks in and only leaves the door open a sliver. The television is just loud enough that I can't hear anything they say. My cheeks heat from embarrassment.

"I cannot believe you had Rylan go in there," I say through my teeth, seething.

"I have to make sure you're safe."

"You are aware that Carey could beat the shit out of Rylan, right?"

She puts her hand on my forearm. "It'll be fine. I'm not worried about that. Hopefully they'll just come to an understanding that as long as he's staying here, he needs to be respectful."

I roll my eyes. "I should've had you leave immediately. You're making this situation so much worse."

It wasn't so long ago that we were in very different places. I was where she is, in love and starting a new chapter in my life. She was where I am—except Rylan didn't die, they just broke up. All the nights I held her when she cried, her complaining about why it was all so complicated. Now, here I am on the other side, and I hate that they all feel I'm so weak that I can't handle this myself.

Rylan comes out and shuts the door. "He's cool. Let's go." Picking up the boxes, he heads to the door.

I want to know every detail of their conversation. Did Carey tell him that we've already met? That I was about to give him my number? That I probably gave him fuck-me eyes at some point?

"What does that mean?" Calista asks.

"I explained that Brinley is the cousin of my wife and you both come from a huge family that protects each other like mama bears, so he should watch his step. I also informed him that he won't be able to go a block without running into one of you Baileys and word is probably already making the rounds that Brinley has a guy room-mate and he should expect to be questioned every time he leaves this apartment."

"We are not that bad." Calista frowns.

I share a smile with Rylan as he says, "Yes, you are. And hey, I come from a big family too. I guess that's why I understand it. Now, can we please go christen our new house?" There's a whine to his voice that makes me laugh.

Calista wraps her arms around me. "You'll call me if you need me?"

I nod against her shoulder. "Go. Have sex."

She tightens her arms so hard you'd think I was leaving for years. "Love you."

"Love you too." I push her back. "Now go!"

They leave the apartment, and as soon as the front door shuts, Carey's bedroom door opens.

VAN

I try to strip the smile off my face, but having her cousin's husband warn me off is too fucking cute for me not to find it humorous.

Rylan said they'd be leaving right away, so I listened by my door. As soon as the apartment door shut, I opened my door, not wanting to give Brinley time to hide out in her bedroom. I definitely catch her off guard because her back is plastered to the front door and her gaze ping-pongs everywhere but on me.

"Can we talk?" I ask.

She pushes off the door and steps forward. She's dressed more relaxed today, in pants that hug her ass and a short sweatshirt. Her blonde hair, thrown up in a messy bun, makes me want to release it to see her long strands fall around her face.

"I'm so sorry. I didn't ask him to do that. They're all just so... protective." There's more she's not saying, but I don't get a chance to ask because she continues. "I wish I could tell you that will be the last time someone says something like that if you stay here, but it won't be. I have twenty-five cousins and eight sets of aunts and uncles, my parents, and a younger brother who, thankfully, is in college right now. Going in there... Rylan did it for Calista because he'll do anything to make her happy, but it was uncalled for and I'm sorry."

I chuckle and walk over to the couch. "When you say if, is that because *you* want me to leave because you thought I was a woman?" I sit on the couch but don't ask her to join me. I want to see if she will on her own.

She sits in the chair next to the couch. "I didn't even think about Carey being a guy's name too. And truthfully, I'm in shock."

"First of all, call me Van. It's my middle name and I've always preferred it over Carey. Also, if you want me to leave, I will. You shouldn't be uncomfortable in your own home."

She crosses her legs and fiddles with the edges of her sweatshirt sleeves, staring at them. "Why did you act like you didn't know me?" Her gaze rises and meets mine.

I feel sucker punched because I see a small amount of hurt in her eyes, as though it would bother her if I didn't remember her.

I shrug, playing off how much the idea of hurting her affects me. "Honestly, you seem like someone who keeps things close to the chest and I figured maybe you didn't want them to know we met a couple days ago. I'll admit, it was a lucky surprise to find out your name and that I might be sharing an apartment with you."

"Nothing can happen now." She shakes her head just in case I don't understand English, I guess.

"Okay."

"No. I mean it." She unwinds her legs and stands. "I'm not like that. That wasn't me that afternoon." She disappears into the kitchen, and I want to follow her, but I don't.

"I said okay," I call to her.

She returns with two bottles of water, holding one out for me. I accept it before she sits back down in the chair.

"I'm sorry, you probably think I'm crazy. I feel crazy sometimes," she mumbles.

I shake my head. "I don't think you're crazy."

"To be honest with you, you're the only one who answered the ad. My cousins said it came off a little anal."

"Well, I answered." In truth, if I'd had another option, I wouldn't have, but I didn't. Then again, if I'd known she'd be my new roommate, I wouldn't have hesitated to answer it in the first place.

She leans back in the chair. "If you want to stay, please do. But I understand if you want to leave."

"I don't."

Her eyes lock with mine, then they slide down to my arms covered in tattoos.

"Who was the guy? On the street that day, outside the tattoo shop," I add when she gives me an odd look.

"Oh, my dad." She bites her lip.

"Really?" I never would've suspected.

"He owns the tattoo parlor."

It takes me a minute, but I put it all together in my head. "Liam Kelly is your dad? I thought you were a Bailey?" I ask, going off what Rylan said.

"My mom is—was before she married. She's a Kelly but still goes by Bailey at her job because it's Bailey Timber." Her forehead scrunches up. "How do you know my dad?"

I huff. "He's the best tattoo artist in Alaska. A lot of my... friends have gone to his shop."

"But not you?"

"Nope. Sadly." I open my water and take a long sip of it. "So, are we going to do this? Live together?"

"Sure. If you still want to?"

"I do."

She places her water on the table and holds out her hand. "Well then, welcome to Lake Starlight. I'm Brinley Kelly."

"Carey Van Adler, but call me Van."

We shake hands and I can't help but notice how soft and silky smooth her skin is. Instantly my mind travels to the image of it wrapped around my dick, but I push that thought away because it's clear that if I stay as her roommate, she's off-limits to me. And she's wise to erect that barrier because I can tell she's not a one-night stand girl. She's a "marry me and have kids with me" kinda girl and I am definitely not in a headspace for that.

"Do you mind if I take a shower?" I stand from the couch, water in hand.

"It's all yours. I cleared out the drawers on the right-hand side and there's a spot for your shampoo and stuff in the shower."

"You have everything handled, huh?" I ask, staring at her.

The cutest blush appears on her cheeks. She's going to be a temptation while I'm here.

"Sorry. Anal, remember?" She chuckles a bit and raises her hand.

I'm not even going to get into the image *that* little phrasing puts into my head.

"I have to go to the grocery store after I've showered. Can I make you dinner tonight as a thank-you for letting me stay even though I'm not who you expected?"

"Um..."

"It's just dinner, Brinley, nothing else."

Her shoulders relax. "Sure. And if you want, I can drive

you to the grocery store. I mean, you probably can't get very many groceries on that motorcycle."

"That'd be great. Sadly, I'll be back in my truck in a day or two. I was already pushing it riding it today." Her head tilts, so I add, "I towed my bike here with my truck. Truck and trailer are parked just outside of town, but I'm gonna have to put her away for the season. Just couldn't resist today when the sun came out for a bit."

"Sounds like you really like your motorcycle."

"She's a good ride." I realize how that sounds coming out of my mouth and clear my throat. "I won't be too long in the shower."

I go to my room and grab my towel, shampoo, and body wash before heading into the bathroom. Something tells me if I leave her alone for too long, she'll be all up in her head and change her mind.

BECAUSE I WAS in such a hurry, I didn't take any clothes into the bathroom with me. When I come out of the bathroom with just a towel wrapped around my waist, Brinley walks out of her bedroom. We stand only inches apart while her eyes soak me in. A strangled sound escapes her throat that makes my dick twitch. I can only hope she doesn't notice.

"Rules. We need rules." She rushes down the hall.

I follow her to a whiteboard on the wall by the kitchen. I figured it was for a grocery list, but I guess I'm wrong because she picks up a dry-erase marker and writes "Rules," followed by the number one below it.

"You should go get dressed." She eyes me over her shoulder and inhales a deep breath.

"Sorry, forgot to take clothes in with me."

She doesn't turn around, putting up her hand. "It's okay, I mean, we should've discussed this kind of thing when we found out that it was a coed situation."

She writes.

1. Must be dressed at all times.

"I prefer to air dry, but okay?"

Her mouth hangs open.

I can't help but chuckle. "I'm kidding. I'll make sure to abide by rule number one."

I head back to my room and strip off my towel. My dick is already half-chub. These next couple of months are going to be full of sexual tension, I know it. I dress in a pair of jeans and a T-shirt, then throw on my leather jacket. I decide on a backward hat instead of actually styling my hair.

"Thank you," she says when I return to the kitchen.

"Sorry again."

"I just want this to work out. I need half of the rent paid and you need a place to live, so we're both stuck. If we started something, it would obviously just be a hookup type of situation and things always go south after a hookup."

Intrigued by her statement, I ask what's forefront in my mind. "Do you do hookups a lot?" Based on how she acted when we met, I wouldn't have thought so, but her words suggest otherwise.

That blush strikes her cheeks again, except this time, it travels up from her neck to her face. "Yeah, of course."

I nod slowly, not really believing her. "And you assume if something happened between us, it would only be a hookup? Why is that?" My head tilts.

She won't look at me as she puts on her coat and zips it,

repositioning her ponytail. "I guess I assumed you were only in town for a short period of time, so you'd only be interested in that."

Smart girl. "Right. It's not because you think I'm a manwhore who doesn't do commitment."

"No." She shakes her head as if she's convincing herself as much as me. "Of course not."

I lean in close, invading her space and whisper, "Maybe you're right." I open the door to the apartment. "Ready?"

She stops at the doorway and looks up at me. "Good thing we have rules, so we don't cross those lines."

I can smell her perfume and I want to soak that scent into my skin. What must it be like to fuck someone like her? Someone so prim and proper. I'd love to pull out another side of her, hear her scream and boss me around as she tells me exactly how to make her come.

Damn it. I shift my stance. I gotta get rid of this half-chub.

She hands me the key as we leave the apartment, and I lock it up then signal for her to go down the stairs first. She unlocks her SUV with the key fob. Once we're inside, I'm surprised to hear her listening to "Feel Like Makin' Love" by Bad Company.

"That surprises me," I say, putting on my seat belt.

She points at the seat belt. "That makes two of us."

"Safety first? So, you're a classic rock fan?" I thought I'd be tortured by some pop music diva the whole way to the grocery store.

"Thank my dad. Although I do like other types of music as well."

I turn it up. "Interesting."

She drives cautiously to the grocery store, making

complete stops at every stop sign, looking both ways at the intersections. I've never felt so safe.

"I'll Stand by You" by The Pretenders comes on and she sings softly, knowing every word by heart. The SUV feels like a cocoon, warm and cozy, with her voice ringing through it. I'm pretty sure she doesn't even know she's singing, and I look out the window so I don't give away that I'm listening to her. I'm sure she'd stop if she knew I noticed.

The lyrics to the song bring out a feeling I wasn't expecting—loneliness. It's been years since I haven't felt alone in this world. Hell, isn't that why my commander made me take a leave of absence before I re-up into the service again? He thinks I need a life outside of the Coast Guard, but he's wrong. The Coast Guard *is* my life.

She pulls into the brightly lit parking lot of the grocery store and doesn't bother going up and down the rows to find the closest parking spot. Instead, she parks in the first spot she finds. We file out of her SUV and walk toward the entrance, but she stops suddenly.

"Shoot," she mumbles.

"Brin?" A woman who looks like an older version of Brinley rushes over with a cart full of groceries.

Brinley glances at me and back at the woman with a resigned look on her face. "Hey, Mom."

five

BRINLEY

My mom's gaze doesn't stray from Van. She looks him up and down, popping a grape from the bag into her mouth.

"Mom," I say to remind her that I'm here too.

She blinks and smirks, turning her attention to me. "Who's your friend?"

"This is Van." I motion to him with my hand out as if she hasn't already been ogling him.

He approaches her, dodging the shopping cart. "Hello, Mrs. Kelly. I'm Van Adler."

"Van Adler, huh? Are you the man my husband mentioned?"

Van side-eyes me and I inhale a deep breath. "We're just getting groceries," I say to change the subject.

"Oh." She puts another grape in her mouth. "So, are you two dating?"

I feel as though I'm thirteen again at my first boy-and-girl dance and my mom just walked in and separated me from Jeremy Schmidt, putting a pillow between us.

"Mom..." I warn, but she smiles, clearly thinking this is

funny. I should've driven us to Greywall to get groceries so we'd be away from everyone.

"I'm just wondering. You told your dad that you were just showing Van to Lucky's and now I find you two in the parking lot of the grocery store." Her perfect eyebrows rise and my shoulders slump.

Although it's the weekend, she's dressed as if she came from the office. She probably did. Since my dad isn't with her, I know he's probably working, and she hates being home by herself.

"Funny thing." I glance at Van to make sure he's up for this, but he has no way to prepare. He clearly doesn't come from a big family, based on the comments he's made, and he has no one here to ridicule him for his decision to move in with me. "Van answered my roommate ad."

A grape falls from my mom's fingers to the ground. Her eyes shift between Van, his tattooed arms, and me. "Oh."

"I would like to point out that even though you all thought my ad was anal, I got someone." I motion toward Van.

"Okay." She seals up the grapes and grows serious when she looks at me. "Brin, may I have a word? You'll excuse us, Van, won't you? It'll only be a moment." She's surprisingly polite.

"Sure, I'll go in and start shopping." Van turns toward me. "Anything you're allergic to?"

I shake my head.

"I'll see you in there." He turns toward my mom. "It was very nice meeting you, Mrs. Kelly." He puts his hand out between them and she shakes it.

"Please, call me Savannah. Welcome to Lake Starlight."

Van beams, showing off his white teeth and my lips tilt up until I look at my mom and my small smile drops.

As he walks through the doors, my mom heads to her SUV, popping open the back door. "Tell me what is going on."

I stuff my hands in my pockets. "I told you. He's my roommate."

"And?" She places a few bags in the back.

"And nothing. He's renting Calista's old room, that's all."

She nods, straightens, and closes the back of her SUV. "We don't know anything about him."

"First of all, *you* don't need to know anything about him. He's nice. And besides, Rylan talked to him."

Her head rears back. "Did he?"

I nod. "I picked him and Calista up from the airport. Van arrived while they were there. So… as embarrassing as it was, Calista made Rylan give him a talk about how to treat me." I chuckle, but she doesn't.

Instead, she takes my hands. I stare at her perfectly manicured nails and soft hands. I've always wanted to be like her, but can't help but feel as though I'm always just shy of her level of perfectionism.

"Your dad isn't going to like this. He didn't like seeing you with him on the sidewalk the other day, and now when he finds out the two of you are living together—" She winces.

"We're roommates, not lovers living together."

Her gaze veers to the grocery store and back to me. "That man isn't going to stay platonic for long."

"You're stereotyping him. You're stereotyping a man who looks just like Dad."

She sighs because she has no rebuttal. "I knew your dad my entire life."

"So what?" I shrug.

"I just want to make sure you're ready for someone like him."

"What does that mean?" My voice grows louder.

A few people heading to their cars turn around. My mom tugs on my arm to situate us on the other side of her SUV, blocking us from staring eyes.

"We don't know anything about his family. What kind of guy is he? Why's he in Lake Starlight? And the thought of you sleeping in the room next to him..." She blows out a breath. "You're just so fragile."

I rip my hands from hers. "I am not fragile," I say through clenched teeth. "I can handle myself. He passed all the background checks. I need a roommate and he needs an apartment. You and Dad wanted me to move on, and I am."

Her head rears back as if I slapped her. "Brinley," she says with her last thread of patience. My mom is used to getting what she wants. I turn to walk away, but she grabs my arm. "What is with you?"

"Everyone treats me with kid gloves. And yes, I'm not entirely comfortable with it because I've never lived with a man other than our family members and Sawyer, but I'm doing it because I need a roommate and I need to move on at some point. I am not fragile."

My mom's hand drops. "Sweetie, you don't have to live with a strange man to show everyone you're moving on. Let your dad handle this. You can come home and live with us while Van stays at the apartment."

"Mom." I sigh and stare at my feet as an orange leaf blows past in the cool breeze.

"It's just..." She doesn't say anything more and my gaze lifts to look at her. "Nothing." She shakes her head. "You're right." She cradles my cheek as she often does when she wants to convey her love for me. "This is your life, and you need to live it. So... please tell Van that I'm sorry if I came off harsh, I was just surprised. But if you need anything, you call."

"Are you going to tell Dad?"

She purses her lips. "I have to, but I'll try my best to convince him to stay out of your business."

I wrap my arms around my mom, and she holds me just as tight.

"Thank you," I say.

Her hand runs up and down my back. "It's going to be in BuzzWheel though, with you two parading around the grocery store." She draws back and puts her hands on my cheeks, staring into my eyes. "People want you to be happy, so they're going to convince themselves things are developing between the two of you even if they aren't. You should prepare him for that."

The town's anonymous gossip app will probably have a picture of us within days if it doesn't already.

I nod even though I'm not sure I want to say anything to him about the app. Maybe it's better if he never discovers it and sees what people say about us on there.

She kisses my forehead. "Well, go on in there, sweetie."

My mom is the one who usually calls the shots on what we do with our lives, so I'm not sure why she's being so easy on this one with me. I'm surprised she didn't call movers right away and have me moved out.

"Also, expect a visit from your dad," she says, climbing into her SUV. "Love you, Brin."

"Love you, Mom."

She shuts the door and starts the SUV while I walk toward the grocery store. I could easily get myself out of this situation, but I don't want to. It's time to reincorporate myself into the world of the living.

Van is in front of the meat section, his cart filled with a mix of junk food and healthy food, not much in between.

"So, what are you making me for dinner?" I ask, surprising him as he pulls a pack of chicken from the bottom of the stack.

"You mean your mom hasn't hired someone to evict me?"

I shake my head. "She's fine, just needs to remember that I'm an adult."

He laughs. "She's protective. She's your mother. She's supposed to be." He pushes the cart to the freezer section, grabs a container of Ben & Jerry's Netflix & Chill'd, and drops it in the cart.

"Ice cream?" I glance in his cart. "Three different kinds of chips, cookies, chocolate milk?"

He stops and stares at me with a really mean look. "Are you judging me?"

"No, not at all. I'm just surprised because you're so..." I motion down his body with my hand. *Jesus, Brinley.*

"What?" He smirks and widens his legs without removing his hand from the cart.

"Just so... oh, come on, you know you're in shape. I figured that was the byproduct of protein shakes and a million sit-ups a day."

He laughs and pushes the cart again. "The sit-ups are real, push-ups too. But I don't have to be so strict with my diet right now, so I'm going to take advantage."

My head tilts. "Why's that?"

He stops again as though I've caught him off guard. "Let's talk about it when we get back to the apartment." He glances around.

Now I'm worried about what he has to tell me. "Okkkaaayy."

He chuckles. "Stop thinking I'm going to say something bad. I promise you the background check was on me even though you thought I was a woman. I've never been in jail for more than a night." He winks, suggesting what you'd assume—that a big guy like him has gotten into a bar fight. "My credit is good." He squeezes my shoulder and a million butterflies set off inside my stomach. "You have nothing to worry about."

I step away from him and his hand drops.

"Sorry."

I shake my head. "It's fine."

We walk side by side down the aisles and he doesn't put much more food into the cart, but when we reach the alcohol, he glances at me. "Are you a red or white kinda girl?"

"Either's fine."

He pulls down one of each and puts them in the cart.

"You don't have to do that," I say.

"I'm making you dinner and that comes with a drink."

"Okay. But you don't have to make me dinner either."

He clicks his tongue on the roof of his mouth. "You say that now, but wait until after I cook for you. Then you'll be asking me to cook all the time."

I smile. "Aren't you full of yourself."

He leans in close as we get to the checkout counter. "There's a big difference between being confident in who you are and what you bring to the table and being conceited."

My lips tingle at the proximity of his. All I want to do is turn my head and find his mouth. How simple that used to be for me, but he's not my boyfriend or even a guy I'm dating.

I help him put the food on the conveyor belt while the cashier scans the items, looking at Van more than what she's ringing through. The bagging girl isn't much better, asking about our night and what we're up to. I'm guessing she's only really asking Van.

"Just bringing these groceries home," he says politely.

As we walk away, I hear my name coming off the bagging girl's lips. I might not know her, but she knows me. That's the curse of a small town. Everyone knows everything.

Thankfully, Van doesn't say anything or ask any questions. We put the grocery bags in the back of the SUV, then I drive us back to the apartment. I glance down the street at Smokin' Guns Tattoos because I expect my dad to be on our doorstep when we arrive home, but no one is hanging around.

"Don't you have to work tonight?" I ask Van as we grab the groceries.

"Nate gave me the night off to get settled but did say it would be the last weekend night I'd get off for awhile, so we better make it a good one. Hence the Netflix and chill."

My mouth hangs open as I head up the stairs. "You think we're going to Netflix and chill?"

"Well, I am more than you, but I'm a sharer, so you can have some too."

I unlock the door to our apartment. "Presumptuous, don't you think?"

He laughs and shakes his head, stepping into our apartment. "Do you suffer from short-term memory loss?"

"What?"

"I'm talking about the ice cream I bought." His eyebrows rise in question.

My phone rings before I can answer, and I see that it's Easton. I should really ignore the call, but I need a distraction right now, so I answer anyway.

VAN

I unpack the groceries as Brinley answers her phone.

Opening the fridge, I crack a smile, looking over my shoulder at the blonde walking away down the hall. Every item already in the fridge is labeled with her name on it. I shake my head. I shouldn't have expected anything different. Not that I'm going to make a tidal wave out of this, but it's funny as hell. What would she do if I ate her yogurt?

It takes me a little while to find my way around her kitchen, but I locate everything I need and prep the dinner. I'm cutting up the chicken to put in the pan when she comes back in, plugging her phone into the charger on the counter.

"Sorry, that was my cousin." She looks over my shoulder, then sits on the counter in the corner of the kitchen.

"Word gets around fast, huh?"

She laughs. "Yeah, although this is Easton, the one who thought I should've brought you home with me the other day."

I side-eye her and again, her cheeks flush pink. "Imagine if you had?"

"Then you probably wouldn't be making me dinner because I wouldn't have let you move in with me."

I put the chicken in the skillet and throw away the scraps I didn't use, then I wash my hands in the sink. She's close to the sink and watches me soap my hands before she leans over and grabs a paper towel off the spool, handing it to me.

"Thanks."

"You're welcome." She's as sweet and welcoming as she is standoffish. Her legs swing back and forth, and her hands are tucked under her thighs. "So, you cook, huh?"

"When you live by yourself, fast food or takeout gets old fast. I started fiddling with recipes, ones that wouldn't take much time." I flip the chicken and chop up the rest of the ingredients. "It doesn't take much."

"I wouldn't know. I'm not a good cook." She jumps off the counter. "Want a glass of wine?"

"I'd love one."

She opens the bottle of white wine, pours a glass for each of us, and hands me one. I pretend to swirl it and smell it before taking a small taste.

"Seriously, is this another thing I'm finding out about you?" she asks.

"I'm kidding. I wouldn't know a good wine over a bad one, but I've had this one before. That's why I picked it."

"Impostor!" She laughs.

While I cook, she clears off the dining table that I'm guessing doesn't get used a lot since there are some books and magazines on the surface. It's not cluttered, but it's not meticulous either.

She has a story, I'm sure of it. Especially with how

protective the people who love her are. Her mom did not look happy to see me next to her tonight.

"My—" She looks at me as if someone just broke in and there's a gun pointed at her temple.

"Who?" She was obviously going to mention someone.

She sighs. "There's something you should know about me. It won't take you long to find out once people get word that you're my roommate anyway."

I put down the stirring spoon. From her body language, I can tell this is something she's either worried to share with me or wishes she didn't have to. I'm not going to take her trust lightly and I don't want her to feel pressured, so I continue cooking dinner without giving her all my attention.

"What is it?" I ask as though I could take or leave her answer when really, I'm near desperate to know what she's going to say.

"Well... I was married. Years ago. I was going to say he loved wine and was trying to teach me. He always laughed and said that I was more of a beer girl like my dad. Which is true."

Jesus, she was married young. But there's real pain in her eyes, so I don't bother inquiring into that facet of her story. I find myself wanting to wrap my hands around the throat of whatever asshole hurt her so badly.

"I'm sorry it didn't work out."

She opens her mouth but shuts it right away. "It's why some people are kind of protective of me around here. They're afraid I'll get my heart broken again."

I nod. "I can see that. If you were my cousin or sister, I'd feel the same way."

Once she turns to set the table, I stir the chicken mixture again. Grabbing the premade salad kit from the fridge, I prepare that, and once I'm finished, she takes the bowl to the table.

We work in silence until she disappears into the bathroom for a few minutes, emerging with red-rimmed eyes. I'm just putting the plate of chicken on the table when she walks past me.

I grab her wrist lightly. "I'm really sorry your first marriage didn't work out. I'll tell you something about myself to make us even."

"You do not need to do that." She tries to slide her wrist out of my grip, but when I run my thumb over the inside, she settles and stays where she is.

"I left home at sixteen and never went back."

Brinley frowns. "Why?"

I release her wrist and shrug. "My stepdad was an asshole and my mom just wanted to make him happy."

"Where are you from?"

"California originally. My mom still lives there."

When she sits down, I take her wineglass and set it on the counter, then I go to the fridge and grab two bottles of beer, opening them and placing one in front of her.

She smiles wide. "Thank you."

"Always feel free to tell me what you want. You could've said something at the store."

Her shoulder lifts. "It's not that big of a deal."

"Maybe we should make a deal?" I cut my chicken and take a bite while she forks her salad first.

"What kind of deal?"

I swallow before responding. "Either we tell each other every horrible thing that's happened in our lives before today, or we sweep it all under the rug and live from today on moving forward."

"You're kidding, right?" She looks at me as though I'm crazy.

"Do you really want to hear about my pathetic upbringing where Santa barely visited? Do you really want to tell me about how your ex did this or that and treated you in a way that makes it look like you've had your heart scooped out when you talk about him? Rehashing all that stuff just makes me feel shitty. How about you?"

She places down her fork and knife. "It does."

"And who wants to feel shitty?"

"Not me." She shakes her head.

"So, deal then?" I put my hand out over the table.

She stares at it for a moment before shaking it. "Deal." She wiggles in her chair. "I like this. So, no personal questions about the past?"

"Nope."

She smiles at her chicken. "Can we make a deal that you cook every day too?"

"Depends," I say. "Are you going to keep labeling your food?"

Her cheeks brighten with color.

"It's a good thing you did. I might have forgotten I didn't buy the yogurt."

She laughs and I do too, glad she can take a joke. I'd never be able to live with someone who couldn't.

I feel a little bad that I've coerced her into agreeing that we won't tell each other anything about our pasts, but I'm still keeping it under wraps that I'm only here for eight weeks even though I signed a year lease. If she finds out I work for the Coast Guard, it's a dead giveaway that I have to blow town at some point because no one gets leave for a year.

THE NEXT DAY, I'm behind the bar at Lucky's while Nate takes inventory of the liquor bottles. It's pretty dead, but he said it picks up after five when the lumber mill lets out, then dies a little around dinnertime to about eight.

So I'm buried in my phone, texting a guy in Kodiak to see how things are going. I miss it there. It's where I found my home after leaving my mom. One of the few places I felt qualified to go.

The door of the bar opens and a stream of daylight casts inside the bar. I glance up and shove my phone in the pocket of my pants. I remember this guy and I'm pretty sure he's here for one specific reason—me.

He sidles up to the bar and Nate glances over his shoulder. An alarmed expression gets thrown my way before he turns fully around and offers his hand. "Liam."

Might as well get this over with.

I raise my hand in greeting. "Hey."

Although Brinley favors her mom, I see now that she shares some physical characteristics with her dad. Like her eyes that are so transparent and give away their emotions. Brinley's is usually shyness, embarrassment, or arousal. That last one is always hard for me to ignore. But currently, Liam's eyes tell me he's determined and definitely pissed off.

"Who's your new hire?" Liam asks Nate.

Nate clears his throat. "This is Van Adler. Liam runs the tattoo parlor next door, Smokin' Guns."

I put out my hand and Liam surprises me by shaking it.

"Nice to meet you," I say.

His handshake is stiff and strong and meant to intimidate. I'm not gonna lie, I've never met a woman's dad in my entire life. Not that I'm sleeping with Brinley, but he's here to warn me. Even Nate realizes that.

"Van is a div—"

"I have some friends who like your work," I interrupt, and Nate gives me a quizzical expression.

Liam examines my arms. "Not you though? Where'd you get those done?"

I look at my own arms covered in tattoos. "Here and there. Mostly Anchorage." I'm lying because they were all done in Kodiak, but saying that will be a dead giveaway for what I do.

He stares at them again and raises his gaze to mine, then makes a noise that says he doesn't believe me. I know certain tattoo artists can do certain styles to perfection, but I never got one of Micah's trademark styles. I'm thankful for that right now because Liam would know I'm lying.

"Mind if I have a word with your new hire?" Liam asks Nate.

"No one else for him to serve." He opens his arms out wide.

"Can I get you something?" I ask.

"Beer. Tap. Light."

I'm a little intimidated by this man because, from what I know of most fathers, they're crazy when it comes to their little girls. Just because I haven't ever come across one doesn't mean I haven't heard the stories. I give him his beer and he examines the head, his lips downturned, but he nods as if to say it's okay, not stellar.

"My wife tells me you're my daughter's new roommate now, Van."

"Yes, sir."

"Don't sir me. Liam is fine."

I don't say anything else.

"Tell me something about yourself." He sips his beer, his legs widening, eyebrows raised.

"My name is Van Adler, I'm originally from California, but I haven't been back there in a lot of years. Found my way up here to Alaska and fell in love with it."

"And your dream is to be a bartender?"

I look over my shoulder at Nate, who's shaking his head while trying to act busy. "Not my dream, but it gets me by."

"Gets you by." He scoffs. "Well, my daughter has been through hell and she sure as shit doesn't need someone like you who's only interested in getting in her pants as her roommate. She needs people she can trust who will have her back and keep her standing."

They really do treat her with kid gloves. I think if I ever overstepped, Brinley would have no problem putting me in my place.

"I'm not going to sleep with your daughter if that's what you're afraid of, sir... er, Liam."

He arches an eyebrow. "Are you suggesting my daughter isn't up to your caliber? Do you think she's ugly?" He sips his beer again and this time it's a much bigger gulp.

"No, she's beautiful. I just mean—"

"Listen, Van, I've been around the block plenty of times, just like you. I might not have drifted far from my hometown, but I wasn't really ever looking for commitment until it came to one girl, Brinley's mom. So I'm warning you now, if you don't keep your dick in your pants and my little girl comes out of this whole roommate situation broken-hearted, you'll have me to answer to. And I'm not intimidated by your muscles." He glances at my arms with disgust.

I nod. "You have my word. When it's my time to leave

town, she won't be brokenhearted. My dick will remain in my pants."

He finishes his beer, digs into his pocket, and slams a twenty on the bar top. "Glad we understand each other. And just so you know, I have eyes everywhere in this town. If you're lying to me, I'll find out."

I raise both hands. "Promise."

"We're here!" A man in his early fifties runs in with a guy who looks just like him right behind. They have to be twins. The only difference is that one has slightly longer hair than the other.

"I handled it already." Liam stands, eyes me one more time, and walks over to his friends.

"Oh man, I missed it. You couldn't have waited? I wanted to do the tough uncle role," one says to Liam as the other one is hunched over, catching his breath.

"I ran for nothing," the other one huffs out.

"Hey, Denver. Rome." Nate lifts his hand in greeting.

They both raise their hands. "Good to see you, Nate," one says.

"Hiring the enemy, Nate? You're lucky your back isn't up against that wall," the other says with a laugh.

Nate looks at me. "He's a good guy. You'll figure that out."

"I hope so," Liam tosses over his shoulder. "Let's go." He nods toward the door.

They all file out after each of them looks in my direction.

Once the door shuts, Nate puts his clipboard on the bar. "Why aren't you telling them you're a diver for the Coast Guard? You know how highly they're thought of around here."

I clean Liam's glass rather than look at him. "Because

I've yet to tell Brinley I'm only here for eight weeks and I don't care what her dad or his friends think of me. They can think I'm the scum of the earth if they want. I don't need to use my profession to buy their high opinion of me."

"I don't understand it, but I'll keep it between us if you want."

I nod and place the clean glass with the rest. "Thanks."

Keeping things from Brinley sours my stomach, but I'll be out of her life in eight weeks, soon to be forgotten after that.

seven

The next day, I'm at the office when I get a text message.

Easton: Way to go, you made BuzzWheel

I MOVE from my text messages to the BuzzWheel app, and sure enough, someone snapped a picture of Van and me at the grocery store. I'm surprised it took whoever runs this thing this long to put up the story.

The headline reads, "Looks Like Someone Might Be Moving On… The Question Is Who's The Guy?"

I read the article that says we were seen at the grocery store looking very friendly with one another. All in all, it has no real information and they haven't even figured out who Van is. The comments below don't offer much except for things like "slide over, Brinley," "I'm calling dibs," and a bunch of "I love him already" messages. Apparently, the women in this town like what they see.

And can I blame them? Hell no.

Having dinner with Van last night reminded me of what it's like to have someone in your life. Someone to come home to. Calista was a great roommate, but the two of us did our own thing, drowning in our sorrow so that we didn't offer much companionship to each other except for binge-watching movies and eating raw cookie dough.

"Hey, you." Calista walks into my office. Speak of the devil.

"What are you doing here?"

"Stealing you away for lunch. I already talked to Aunt Savannah, so no excuses." She's glowing—like actually glowing with rosy cheeks and a big smile, all while wearing yoga pants and a sweatshirt with sneakers.

"Must be nice to be the wife of a professional soccer player," I chide, and she shakes her head.

"I have to go over to the sports complex after."

"Look at you." I walk around the desk and grab my coat and purse. "Kicking ass and taking names."

She shakes her head. "Actually, the little one is causing some nausea," she whispers.

"Why are you whispering?"

"Because we haven't gone public yet."

"Calista, you were in BuzzWheel."

I'm so excited for my cousin but she doesn't seem to realize yet that there's no point in trying to keep it under wraps around here. Especially when she accidentally left the positive pregnancy test in the bathroom at the sports complex.

She huffs. "I'm mad at Francie, you know. You'd think that woman to woman she could keep a secret. Anyway, I haven't announced it, and I'm not showing, so… but he or she is starving, so we're going to the pizza place."

"Okay," I say and follow her out of my office.

"See you girls later." My mom waves at us, her ass perched on her assistant's desk, gossiping. "Have fun."

"Thanks, Mom," I mumble.

Calista kisses Mom's cheek before we leave the Bailey Timber building. Walking out of the office, I inhale a deep breath of cool Alaskan air, happy to be out of the stiffness of the office.

"How's work going?" she asks.

We decide on her car since it's closer because she parked along the curb, a.k.a. the fire lane, instead of in an actual spot in the parking lot.

"Meh." I shrug. "I'm not sure all this is for me. Mom said this morning we might have to fire someone."

Calista starts the car and cringes. "Which means…"

I nod. "Yeah, *I* have to fire the someone."

She gives me a pitying look because she knows I don't have my mom's steel spine. Mom said she didn't either when she started and Great-Grandma Dori taught her how to run the business, wisdom she's trying to impart to me. My mom insists that eventually it'll become second nature to me. I disagree, but she doesn't really want to hear that.

Calista drives to the outskirts of town toward her and Rylan's favorite pizza place.

"Is Rylan meeting us?" I ask.

She glances over at the stoplight. "No, why?"

"Because it's, like, your spot."

"Actually, we're going to pick it up. I have something I

want to show you, but first I want you to tell me about Mr. Muscles." She waggles her eyebrows.

I stare out the window at streets I've known my entire life. Sometimes I wonder what's beyond the city limits of Lake Starlight. Sure, I've left for vacation and college, but I've never entertained not living in this town. "There isn't much to say. He cooked me dinner. He's nice. Respectful."

Her relieved smile could light up the biggest stadium. "I'm so happy to hear that. He sounds wonderful."

She parks outside the pizza place and runs in, returning a minute later with pizza and a brown bag that probably contains her favorite breadsticks.

Once she's back in the vehicle, I ask, "Is this going to be a pregnancy craving for you?"

"I think so. This morning, Rylan said no more pizza. He couldn't handle any more."

"So, you're using me to get what you want."

She squeals and squeezes my thigh. "Maybe a little. But just you wait. I can't wait for you to see this surprise I have for you."

I have no idea what she could be surprising me with.

We drive down by the lake to a remote area that used to scare me when I was younger. The woods are heavy and unkempt, there are no walking trails, and the roads are narrow and winding. Easton and Lance used to tell me axe murders lived on this side of town and to make sure I never ventured in.

"Where are you taking me?" I ask, feeling as if we've been driving forever. Not to mention having to smell this pizza the whole way has my stomach grumbling.

"Just wait."

Ten minutes later, she pulls into a gravel driveway that

leads to a house that reminds me of a replica of Hansel and Gretel's house.

"Now I'm scared," I say, staring at the cottage.

"Don't be. Come on." She takes the keys out of the ignition, climbs out, and grabs the pizza, waiting at the front of the car for me to follow.

I warily step out of her car, my high heels sticking in the gravel on my way up to the door. "When are you going to answer my questions?"

"Here, hold this." She passes me the pizza and uses a key to get into the place.

When she opens the door and we step in, it's dark with no light streaming in. I glance to my left and find a picture of a very young great-grandma Dori and great-grandpa Phillip.

"Calista, what is this place?" I stop.

She comes over to stand beside me. "It was theirs, and now it's yours."

I feel as if all the blood drains from my face. What the hell is she talking about?

CALISTA REFUSES to say anything more until we're seated at a small table with the pizza between us. After a few seconds, I stand, deserting my pizza, and inspect the place.

"It was their hideaway," she says around a bite of pizza. "And last year, Alice from Northern Lights met me here with a key for the place. Then this lawyer guy came and handed me a letter from Great-Grandma Dori that said she was leaving the cabin to me. It was all very bizarre."

I whip around, my heart aching with the hope that she

left me a letter too. I've missed Great-Grandma Dori so much in the few years since she passed.

Calista smiles and digs around in her purse before holding up an envelope. "This is yours."

I rush across the hardwood and snag it out of her hold, seeing my name scribbled in Great-Grandma Dori's handwriting. I look up from the envelope. "Oh my god! How did you get this?"

"I knew there would be one waiting for you too. So, I told the lawyer I wanted to give your letter to you." My finger moves to slide under the lip of the envelope, but Calista puts her hand on mine to stop me. "Trust me and read it alone. I'm not sure what yours says, but I know that you should read it alone."

"Okay." I sit back down, but the letter isn't far from my mind. I want to read it so badly.

She slides the key across the table. "Here, take this. It's yours."

I frown. "But I thought you said she left it to you?"

"She said I could do what I want with the cabin, and you need it right now. Being here helped me when everything was going down with Rylan last year. Maybe it was just feeling her presence since she loved it here, I'm not sure, but it helped me to see things differently." She runs her hand over her stomach. "I'm not sure we would be where we are now without this cabin."

I don't say anything for a while, letting her memories take her back.

She finally says, "Anyway, I know Van seems nice, but I also know you didn't want a guy roommate, so now you have this place to hunker down in when you need to get away."

"All those nights you didn't come home, this is where

you really were?" I'd inquire where she was spending the night and she'd make up lame excuses like saying she was at her parents'.

She nods and takes another piece of pizza.

"Huh. Did you change anything?" I look around the small space again.

"No. Rylan mentioned clearing the path to the lake. There's a great view down there, but we never got around to it."

I look around some more at all the pictures of my great-grandma and great-grandpa when they were young and in love. The cottage needs a redo, but it's charming in an odd, nostalgic way. Eventually I venture into the only bedroom and sit on the edge of the bed. It squeaks and groans under my weight and feels as if it's about to break.

Calista comes in a minute later. "Yeah, not very reliable when it comes to sex. *But!*" Her eyes light up and she rushes over to the closet. "Check this out."

Inside are a bunch of foam presentation boards that remind me of something you see on TV when a detective is trying to link all the puzzle pieces of a case together. Only these have pictures of our aunts and uncles and parents when they were around our age.

"Are these what I think they are?" I smile.

Calista nods and pulls out the board for my parents. Written on it is *Get Savannah to stay at Liam's* with a bunch of other stuff written underneath.

"And they gave me hell for moving in with Sawyer before we got married." A soft chuckle leaves my lips as I study it. "These are too funny." I shake my head since these confirm what we've been told all these years—that Great-Grandma Dori and her best friend, Ethel, did indeed have their hands in all our parents getting together.

"I know, right?"

We sit for a while and look through all of the boards and how intricate they are. You'd think Aunt Juno, who is the actual matchmaker in our family, would've been involved, but even she has a board. All the instructions are there to get her to see her best friend Colton as more than a friend.

I'm a mix of emotions when we return the boards to the closet and go back to the table. Being here makes me miss my great-grandma, but at the same time, I know how lucky I was to have her in my life for as long as I did. That gives me a sense of peace.

Calista picks up another piece of pizza and eyes me as she chews.

"I appreciate this, but I'm not sure how often I'll use this place. I mean, the area spooks me and living with Van hasn't been horrible. He actually cooks a lot, and he's cleaner than I am. Just yesterday, he organized my junk drawer."

"That's great! If you don't need this place, that's fine, but know it's here for you. I'd like all of our cousins to find refuge here. I wasn't going to keep it all to myself." She takes another bite of pizza. "Don't give me that look. The baby is hungry, okay?"

I hold up my hands, laughing. "I'm not saying a thing."

We finish the pizza and she takes the box home with us so she doesn't have to come back here to put out the garbage. Once we're back in the car, I look at the cabin again.

"Thanks, Calista," I say.

She tilts her head and studies me, probably trying to figure out what I'm thinking. "Anytime. I'm always here for you. No matter where I live."

I squeeze her hand. "Best cousin award goes to you."

She drops me off at the office, and I anxiously ride the elevator up to my floor, then shut my office door as soon as I'm inside. I'm opening the letter from Great-Grandma Dori before I even sit in my chair.

eight

VAN

For someone with such an anal ad, this girl is anything but neat. I take out the trash since it's filled to the brim. Then I empty the dishwasher and put the dishes away before I make dinner. It's my night off and I'm looking forward to just eating in front of the television and vegging out, so I'm making my chicken fried rice with teriyaki sauce. It's easy to make and perfect to eat in front of the television.

The apartment door opens and Brinley walks in, smiling at me in the kitchen. "You're like a woman's dream. You're always in the kitchen." She slips off her high heels and hooks them in her fingers before walking to her room.

"Are you in tonight?" I ask before she disappears into her room.

"I'm pretty much always in." She laughs and her bedroom door shuts a second later.

I put the rice in the wok pan I found in the cabinet. She has a lot of kitchen stuff I wouldn't think someone her age would have. I was prepared to use a skillet.

A few minutes later, she walks in wearing a pair of

joggers and a shirt that just reaches the waistband of her pants. Her blonde hair is thrown into a messy bun, but her makeup is still on.

"Feel better?" I ask, trying not to make her uncomfortable by staring.

"I'll never get used to having to dress up for work."

"Well, you always look really nice."

Her cheeks pinken. For a second, an image of her naked under me with that flush over her whole body flashes in my mind. I squeeze my eyes shut to erase the image. We've made it clear that neither of us should act on the tension that fills the room whenever the two of us are together.

"Thank you, but what I wouldn't do for a job where I could wear jeans and a T-shirt. Like my dad. The man has it made."

I chuckle. I never told her that her dad came to visit me at work. Didn't seem like she'd appreciate it, and if I were her dad and a guy like me was sniffing around, I'd warn him too.

"Where do you work?" I ask.

She takes two beers out of the fridge and hands one to me as I pour in the sesame oil and soy sauce. "My family owns Bailey Timber, and if you haven't figured it out yet, I'm to take over the company from my mom. She took it over after her parents passed, and I guess I'm the chosen one."

I stir the rice and look at her from the corner of my eye. "And you're not happy about that?"

She shrugs. "I guess at some point I must've said I wanted it. It's just always been the expectation, I suppose. I mean, everyone says I'm like my mom."

"You definitely look like her."

She smiles. "Except the eyes." Brinley points at those

gorgeous blue eyes that reveal everything going on in her head. Although I only saw her dad's eyes full of fury.

"Do you enjoy it?"

She grabs two plates and places them on the counter next to me.

I pick them up and swap them for bowls. "Easier in front of the television."

"Oh, what are you going to watch?"

"I don't really know, but it's my one night off and all I want to do is chill."

Her eyebrows rise.

"Not Netflix and chill, just chill."

She's still a little on edge around me, and all I want is for her to let go of her anxiety about me being her room-mate. It's a little uncomfortable, but I could see us becoming good friends since we've removed the possibility of romantic feelings.

Her eyes are wide as she looks at me.

"Brinley, relax." I use my most reassuring voice.

"I am." Hers comes out high-pitched and squeaky.

"You aren't. You're tense like you think something is going to happen."

She shakes her head and goes into the family room. I peek out of the kitchen and see that she's arranging spots on the chair and couch. God forbid we sit on the same piece of furniture. The divorce must have been brutal with how standoffish she is.

"It's just... I don't know how to explain it." She doesn't say anything more than that.

I spoon the fried rice into two bowls and hook my fingers around the beer bottles, bringing it all into the family room.

She helps by taking the beers and setting them on coasters, then taking her bowl. "It smells delicious."

"Thanks. It's super easy, but it's the teriyaki that makes it so good."

Just as I expected, she sits in the chair with her legs crossed. I sit on the couch, but I purposely pick the corner closest to her.

"How did you ever start cooking?" she asks.

"I told you, takeout—"

She raises a hand. "There has to be something else."

I inhale, wanting to put on the television and forget this line of questioning. We said no personal questions about the past, but I can give her this. "When you don't make a lot of money, it's hard to eat the meals you might want to, so I looked up recipes online. It's cheaper to buy the ingredients and make it yourself."

She smiles and forks her fried rice. "Thanks for being so honest. You didn't have to."

"I'm not ashamed of not having money. I left home young and barely got by, so even when I jo—ended up with a paycheck, I still tend to cook."

"So, you like bartending?"

I chuckle. "We're getting personal."

"You asked me about my job." She points her fork at me.

I chuckle. "True. I like it enough, but it's not my passion."

"What is?" Her blue eyes look at me with avid interest.

I stop eating and stare at her. "I'll tell you when you tell me."

She nods and looks at the TV. "Okay, what are we watching?"

I laugh and she does too since we're both happy to dodge the question, but her not answering proves that my instinct was right—she doesn't want to run her family's company. From what I've gathered working at Lucky's, Bailey Timber employs more than half the town, and the Bailey name means something around here.

Nate told me the other day while I was opening that when Brinley's grandparents died, the nine Bailey siblings varied in age from twenty-two to nine or something. Brinley's mom came back from college to run the company with her grandma Dori, and Brinley's uncle returned from college to raise the younger siblings. Apparently her uncle would've most likely gone pro for baseball but gave it all up. The town thinks of the Baileys as their own kids and treats them and the great-grandchildren much the same. Which just firmed up my idea of not crossing the line with Brinley because if I inadvertently hurt her, the town might come after me with pitchforks.

I grab the remote and turn on Netflix. It's her account that's logged on and I see that she's already started *The Mindy Project,* so I hover over it and look in her direction. "Want to continue this?"

"That's okay. I'm already on season three and there are only six, so..."

I nod. "You could catch me up. I did love her in *The Office,* and it says it's the same writers."

She sets down the bowl of rice and grabs her beer, looking a little solemn all of a sudden. "Truth?"

"Of course."

"I was watching it with my husband. I've tried over and over to get back into it, but I only make it a few minutes in before I turn it off." She shrugs. "Feels weird watching it by myself or something."

My lips press together. "Then it's a done deal. You need new memories of watching it and I happen to be a fun person to watch television with." I click the button to start the show.

A sound comes out of her, but she finishes her beer and goes into the kitchen. "Do you need another one?" she asks, her voice cracking.

"Sure."

She comes out with two beers.

I look at her with concern and pause the show. "I didn't mean to pressure you. If it's too much…"

She shakes her head. "No, I've been wanting to see what happens, and I need to move on, right?"

I smile, feeling proud in a way. It's clear this ex did a number on her, and moving on hasn't been easy. "Damn right you do."

She straightens her back and tucks her legs under her ass, putting the bowl of rice on the arm of the chair. "You can start it again."

The show starts, and she has to tell me who people are and what's happening. We laugh at the same parts and there's a lot more sex talk than I thought there would be, which makes it hard since I haven't had any in a few months. The one couple's sex scene goes on and on, and the longer we sit there, our bowls of rice done and on our third beers, the harder it becomes to ignore the rising tension between us. I have to resituate myself, but if Brinley notices, she doesn't say anything.

"I wish I could be like her," she says about the main character. "She's so sure of herself."

I frown. "Why are you not?"

"I don't know. I think about when I was in high school and how I was then. So confident."

"Lots of teenagers have an inflated sense of ego, I think."

She nods. "I know, but my high school was a small school, and everyone knew everyone. I didn't go to one of those high schools you see in television shows or movies. There wasn't a guy I didn't think I could get."

"And you think there's a guy now that you couldn't get?" I arch an eyebrow.

She looks down her nose at me. "I'm not looking."

"But if you were, you do know you could grab any guy on the street and they'd take you home, right?"

I'm probably stepping over a line here, but I hate seeing women feel insecure. Although it's not my mom's fault that she found herself in a verbally abusive relationship, I believe her insecurity kept her there, convincing her she couldn't do any better. He saw that weakness and doubled down. I tried to get her to leave with me at sixteen, but... I shake my head, clearing the memory.

Brinley is not my mother and doesn't have bad self-esteem. She's just recently divorced and is still working through all that emotional baggage.

"You're sweet and trouble." She points the mouth of her beer bottle at me.

"Trouble?"

She shakes her head and stands, then disappears into the kitchen with our empty bowls. I pause the show and follow her.

"You know exactly why you're trouble. You can't look like you do and be sweet too. It's too much."

I hold up my hands while she rinses the bowls. "You can't blame me for how I look, you'll have to blame God for that one." I lean my hip on the counter with my arms crossed.

A loud laugh falls out of her, then she stares at me. "I didn't take you for being conceited."

"It's not conceit, it's confidence. I have mirrors, and yes, I've been blessed with this amazing face and body, but my personality, that's all me." I'm not really serious. I mean, I'm aware I'm attractive to some, but I'd pick a good personality over a good ass any day of the year.

She turns after finishing with the bowls and stares at me. "Share some of that confidence with me, will you?"

Tension sizzles like a live wire between us. I step toward her, and the room grows smaller. Unable to resist even the smallest touch, I tuck a strand of her hair behind her ear and tip her head up to look at me. Those eyes are begging, pleading for me to make her feel her worth. Show her how attractive I find her. All the talk about how nothing could happen went out the window in the few hours since we sat and watched television.

My hand cradles her head, my thumb running along her cheek. "The first thing I thought when I saw you in the diner was how gorgeous you were. How of course you were at a table with two guys because a woman like you would never be starved for male attention. I wondered if I'd been a half hour earlier if I could've been the guy sitting with you. And when, who I now know is your cousin, kissed you on the forehead, I thought I'd never be able to keep my lips from yours if it were me."

Her shoulders relax. It's as if we're gasoline and someone lit the match. Our bodies lean in, and I bend my head while she rises to her tiptoes. All the doubts vanish when her tongue slides along her lips.

"You're beautiful, so fucking beautiful," I murmur, millimeters away from our lips touching.

Her eyes meet mine and we both breathe heavily, our breath fanning the other's face. The longer our eyes soak in the other, hers transform and all that lust and longing are replaced with trepidation.

She gently pushes me back. "I'm so sorry. I can't."

She runs to her room, and the door slams shut.

With a sigh, I look down at my hardening dick. "Guess we fucked that up."

BRINLEY

There's a soft knock on the door. "I'm really sorry, Brinley," Van says.

"It's okay. Honestly. Just took me by surprise. Sorry for the freak-out," I say from the other side of the door because I cannot face him right now.

"Come out and let's finish watching the show."

"I'm really tired and I need to get up early tomorrow to watch my cousins play basketball. Go ahead and finish it though. I'll catch up later."

My back falls to my mattress, and I cover my head with a pillow. My cheeks burn from embarrassment. What was I thinking, asking him to share his confidence? It's been so long since anyone has done that.

"All right." I hear his sigh through the door. "Get some rest. And again, I'm sorry."

I take the pillow off my face only to flop it back down again.

A normal twenty-five-year-old would be able to handle an almost kiss from their hot roommate. She wouldn't lock herself in her room and freak out. Maybe I am as delicate as my family wants to believe.

I flip over and grab Great-Grandma Dori's letter from my nightstand drawer. It's already becoming worn from the number of times I've read it.

MY DEAREST BRINLEY,

I SO WISH *I could be around to hand you this letter, or hell, to give you the advice firsthand once you were ready to hear it. After Sawyer died, I tried to tell you what I'm writing in this letter, but you were too lost in your grief to listen. You convinced yourself Sawyer was your one true love and compared it to my relationship with your great-grandpa Phillip. What I didn't tell you then was that I had a long life with your great-grandpa. We raised a son together and had many years as empty nesters, babysitting our grandchildren. So, when I lost him, I had all those memories to keep me warm at night. The thought of starting over with someone new after having someone who knew me so well was exhausting. I mean, I spent years training Phillip to put the toilet seat down. He knew my mood from the second he opened the door after work. I didn't want to spend the last of my years training another man because, let me tell you, that's hard work. But, sweetie, you're young. Don't hate me for this, but I often thought you were too young to marry, but that wasn't for me to say.*

I BLOW OUT A BREATH, thinking of all the fights I had with my parents when I announced my engagement at twenty years old. After he died, our fights were me screaming that they were probably happy now. I was such a bitch to them during my angry phase of grief.

With a sigh, I keep reading.

YOU'RE SO YOUNG—A *lot of people are going to come in and out of your life. And you never know if they're important and are going to teach you some life lesson or if they're just passing through. Sometimes the ones you didn't pay much attention to stay in your life, and others you thought would be by your side forever, leave you with memories that eventually fade.*

I beg you, my darling great-granddaughter, to give love another chance. I know what I am asking of you and it's not an easy task. But open that closed heart of yours because it's much too beautiful and genuine to be tarnished and hidden your entire life. There's enough room in there that Sawyer can share, and if he loved you like I think he did, he wants you to be happy again because being loved by you is a true gift.

I leave it in your hands now. Just be open to my words and think them over for however long you need, but I know that one day, a man is going to come into your life and weasel his way into your heart without you realizing it until it's too late. And when you realize it's happened, do not run away, my darling. Stay and fight those demons. Fight for what you deserve—and that is to love and, most of all, to be loved.

LOVE ALWAYS,
   Great-Grandma Dori

. . .

I WIPE AWAY the stray tears, folding the letter and putting it back in the drawer. I'd be crazy to think that Van Adler is the one who'll find his way into my heart since I'm pretty sure he's not into commitment, and he won't be in Lake Starlight forever. From what I've gathered, he doesn't put down roots, and that's the last type of person I need, but maybe he'd be fun to fool around with, sort of ease me back into being with a man again.

Fool around? Come on, Brin, you ran away after he almost kissed you.

What am I thinking?

I hear him go to the bathroom like I have other nights. He has a meticulous nighttime routine. He showers every night and changes into his pajama pants or sweatpants, then returns to the bathroom, where he flosses and brushes his teeth. Goes to the bathroom, washes his hands, then disappears into his bedroom.

So, after the second shutting of his door, I slide out of my room and get ready for bed. When I return, I pack a small bag. I need to get out of here for a little bit.

Although the cabin scares me, Great-Grandma Dori is right—I need to face my fears, and the cabin is one of them. Then again, I fear an axe murderer less than I fear staying in this apartment and sleeping with my new roommate—because what happens after that?

I'VE HOLED myself up at the cabin all weekend. Though it was scary at first, what with all the animal noises an Alaskan girl like me should know, I've grown more comfortable. Mostly because I stopped tormenting myself for acting so juvenile in front of Van.

I'm sure if I told Van I'm a widow, he'd understand, but I don't want another set of those pitying eyes on me. I knew I wouldn't be able to keep Sawyer's name out of my mouth or hide the fact I was married before, so letting him believe I'm divorced seemed easy. I just hope someone in town doesn't tell him. I guess if someone opens their big mouth, I'll deal with it.

With no television, I've spent the weekend listening to music and investigating the cabin, reading all the mission boards that got my aunts and uncles together. My grandma and her best friend knew their shit. It's really amazing how they worked their magic.

A knock on the door startles me and I peek out the curtain to see the Lake Starlight Retirement Community van. That's where my great-grandma Dori and Ethel used to live. I open the door to find Alice, one of the residents there. She walks in with her friend Jean.

"Brinley," Alice coos.

Alice and Jean were Dori and Ethel's friends. Calista tried to convince me last year that they had something to do with getting her back together with Rylan, but truth be told, Calista and Rylan just needed five minutes in a room together. Their sexual chemistry and love for one another took care of the rest.

"Hi, Alice. Hi, Jean." I'm friendly but a little confused as to why they're here.

"I didn't know Calista gave a key to anyone?" Jean looks around as if she's casing the place to come back tonight and break in.

"Um… yeah."

Alice runs her hand down my arm. "Good, that's good. Jean and I usually come and check things out once a week. Make sure no pipes have frozen, or a tree hasn't landed on the cabin. No bear has made his home here." She laughs.

A zip of fear that these are things that could happen races through me. I miss my apartment in downtown Lake Starlight.

"Why are you staying here?" Alice diverts my attention, but I keep one eye on Jean as she ventures into the bedroom.

"Is she looking for something?" I thumb in the direction of where Jean went.

"Just checking that everything's okay. So, what have you been up to? How is Bailey Timber?" She pulls out a kitchen chair and sits.

I step back to check on Jean and she walks out of the bedroom and goes outside.

"Well?" Alice pulls my attention back to her.

"It's good. All good." I give her a small smile.

"Then why are you here? We saw your hunk of a roommate."

"At Lucky's?"

She waves as if it doesn't matter. "I assume your parents are mad."

Jean comes in then, and they share a look.

"Well, we should get going. Rude of us to intrude. If you have any problems, don't hesitate to give us a call." Alice hands me a business card that just has her name and phone number on it.

"Okkaayy," I say and push it into the back pocket of my jeans.

I walk them out and hover by the door to watch them leave. They wave before climbing into the van. The driver pulls out of the driveway and honks as they drive away.

It isn't until an hour later, and I have two blankets over

me, that I realize something is wrong. I check the thermo-stat, and it says it's sixty-five when last night I turned it to seventy-two. I press the button again to raise the tempera-ture, but I don't hear the furnace kick on. Going over to the back closet where the furnace is, I see a metal piece on the floor.

I bend and grab it, holding it up. "I'd bet money this is Jean!"

I don't want to bother Calista with this. She and Rylan should be happy and living in bliss, not dealing with furnace issues, so I decide to take care of it myself. I call the number on the furnace and the guy's wife tells me he'll be out after she feeds him lunch.

Great.

Two hours later, a van with a furnace company name I'm not familiar with pulls into the driveway. I thought I knew all the businesses around here. Then again, if Great-Grandma Dori was trying to keep this place a secret, she wouldn't use a Lake Starlight business.

"The name is Joe." The older man in jean overalls and boots looks around the small cabin. "So, the furnace isn't working?"

I walk him over to the unit, but he seems familiar with it. As he works, I try to give him space, but when he stands, wipes his face with a handkerchief, and sighs, I know he's about to tell me bad news. I thought he'd come and fix it, and maybe I'd continue to stay here until Van Adler is out of Lake Starlight, like the chickenshit I am.

"You have another place to stay?" he asks, which is a telling way to start the conversation.

"I have an apartment in Lake Starlight."

"I have to order the part. Not sure what happened or

how it just came off, but with a furnace this old, it's going to take a few weeks."

I sigh. "There's no way to get it sooner?"

"No, I have to wait for the part. But I'll make some calls. It might come faster. Leave me your number on the back of my card and I'll call you as soon as I have news."

I scribble my cell number on the back and pass it back to him. He slides it into the front pocket of his overalls.

"How much do I owe you today?" I ask.

He waves me off with his handkerchief. "Nothing. Let's wait until the part comes in and we'll square away then."

I nod. "Thank you so much for coming out here today."

He smiles. "Don't mention it." I walk him to the door, and he turns around. "You can't stay here tonight. The weather is making a turn, and you'll freeze to death."

I hold up my hands. "I have plans to go back to my apartment."

"Good. That's a good decision."

I watch his van pull out of the driveway before I pack up my stuff and suck up the fact I have to come face-to-face with Van again.

VAN

Lucky's is crazy busy, but it doesn't keep my mind off the fact that I pushed Brinley out of her own apartment. She hasn't been home in two nights. It's now Sunday, and as all the patrons watch football on the TVs, I'm left wondering where she went and how many people in this bar might know exactly what happened.

It took me a few days to realize that in Lake Starlight, people know you or things about you even if you don't know them. It took a couple more to figure out part of the reason why—the BuzzWheel app that keeps everyone in town in everyone's business.

A woman approached me and said, "So you're Brinley Kelly's new roommate, huh?" When I answered yes, she proceeded to look me up and down and said, "Where did they find you? You'll get her out of her hole, that's for sure."

I had so many questions, but it felt weird to ask a stranger rather than Brinley.

When she asked why I came to town, I told her it was because of the awesome snowmobile trails they have. It's a hobby I picked up once I got to Kodiak. I don't think I'll ever move to warmer weather.

As I'm serving the Northern Lights Retirement table their coffees and another bowl of nuts, Brinley's cousins I saw her with at the diner, enter the bar. They have Rylan and Calista with them. Piling into a recently vacated booth, the one who I thought was Brinley's husband raises his hand for me, so I head over.

"Hey, Van, right?" he asks.

I nod.

"I'm Easton, this is Lance, and you know Calista and Rylan, right?"

I nod at Calista and Rylan. "Nice to see you again." Then to the blond guy, I say, "Nice to meet you too. What can I get you guys?"

"Four beers." Easton holds up four fingers as though I don't speak English.

If I knew him better, I'd razz him, but I don't, and I've done enough to their family, what with Brinley running away.

Calista clears her throat.

"Shit, sorry, three beers and a kiddie cocktail?" Easton says.

Calista narrows her eyes. "Just a water for now."

"I'll be right back."

On my way to the bar, I take a few more orders. Usually the waitstaff handles the booths, but Nate had two of them call in sick with a stomach bug this morning. The tips will be nice though, since I might be shacking up at the Glacier Point after all. I refuse to drive Brinley out of her own apartment.

When I return to the booth, the one grandma with red hair, Alice, is chatting with Calista and Rylan about baby stuff. I guess she must be pregnant, but she doesn't look it at all.

"Alice, they do not need a baby shower. Do you know how much Rylan makes?" Easton says.

Alice turns to him and must give him some look because his eyes widen. "The point of a shower is to welcome the baby. It's not just about the gifts. I swear, Easton Bailey, you'll be single forever."

"What do a baby shower and me being single forever have to do with one another?" His forehead wrinkles.

"Why do you antagonize everyone?" Calista asks him. "Alice was being nice, offering to knit something and maybe host the shower at Northern Lights." She shakes her head.

"And will you please stop telling people how much I fucking make? You don't even actually know."

I set down the beers, and Easton raises his and tips it at Rylan before taking a swig. "Us professional athletes know these things."

"Neither one of you has the money Lance does anyway," Calista chimes in with a grin.

Lance says nothing, but his cheeks turn a slight shade of pink that reminds me of Brinley. Rylan blows out a breath as it clicks in my head who these guys are. Rylan is a professional soccer player, and Easton is a professional baseball player.

"And we're so fortunate our off seasons align," Easton says, clinking his bottle against Rylan's, who doesn't really reciprocate.

When all their eyes turn in my direction, I realize I've been standing here listening, and since I'm literally staring at them all like a dumbass, I figure I'll ask the burning question in my throat. "Have you guys talked with Brinley lately?"

Calista gets fidgety, sipping her water. Easton and Lance look at one another and shrug, shaking their heads.

"Why?" Lance asks.

"Well." I clear my throat.

"I did." Calista quickly raises her hand.

"Why are you raising your hand?" Easton asks.

I can tell he's the kind of guy you either love or hate and not much in between.

Calista lowers it. "She had a big project and has been at her parents', working with her mom. She said she left you a note."

She's the worst liar I've ever met. Seriously, her fingers are twisting in her lap, and her eyes look in every direction but mine.

"Yeah, she did. It just didn't say when she'd be back."

"Tonight," a voice from the booth next to us says. Alice stands. "I saw her this afternoon, and she'll be back tonight."

Calista's eyebrows furrow. "Really? I thought it was going to take longer?"

"Nope, Jean and I had to make a visit over where she's staying this afternoon, and she told us as much."

I'm way too new in this town to understand all the dynamics, but if Alice wants to throw a baby shower for Calista and knit something for her baby, I'd say she must be a good friend of the family. So I have no reason not to believe her, even if Calista seems skeptical.

"Great. Thanks. Although I probably won't be home until she's asleep." I walk away from the table and fill my orders.

An hour later, my break comes. Instead of staying in the

bar, I go out and walk along the back of the building to clear my head.

AFTER WE'RE closed and have cleaned up the bar, Sabrina, another bartender, and I walk out. She locks the door since I'm still waiting for Nate to get me a key.

"What a killer night, huh?" Sabrina has short, dark hair and thick bangs with makeup on the heavier side, but she's attractive, especially in her short skirt and too-small T-shirt. If she worked at a bar by the base, I probably would've already hit on her. But I know better than to fuck a coworker.

"Yeah, I'm beat."

She clicks her fob, and a small sedan down the street beeps. "I was going to ask if you were game to go to a bar on the outskirts of town. It's a biker bar and they're open late. You'd fit right in."

Her hand runs down the arm of my jacket, an arm that holds tattoos that probably make her think that. Her bright-green eyes are full of lust. If she was a customer... maybe, but she's a coworker. Besides, I already have a set of baby blues I can't get out of my head.

"Sorry, another time. I'm beat." I'm mostly tired from staying up late and waiting for Brinley to come home. Her whole story of a work project and going home is bullshit, and all I want to do is apologize and tell her it won't happen again.

"Okay, but I'm a great dancer." She smiles and walks away.

I wait at the curb for her to climb into her car. Once she drives off, I walk down the sidewalk toward the apartment.

It's eerily quiet since we're the last business open in Lake Starlight. Smokin' Guns is dark, and so are the diner and all the other restaurants and shops. But it's nice, the quiet of a small town at night. Kodiak had a few rare nights like this, but too much happens on the water at all times of the day for it to be quiet like this. I fight the urge to walk to the lake and instead use my key to open the apartment door.

When I walk into the apartment, the kitchen stove light is on, but nothing else is. I smell her perfume, and it's fresh, so I know she's returned. That shouldn't make my heart race or fill my body with peace, but it does. She's not mine. I've known her for a week, for Christ's sake.

There's another note on the dry-erase board right under rule number one.

VAN,

I'M HOME. *Thanks for keeping the place so tidy. See you in the morning.*

Brin

I'VE NOTICED a lot of her cousins and her parents refer to her as Brin, but I haven't felt comfortable shortening her name yet. Shortening someone's name feels intimate, or like you've known that person for years, know their darkest secrets. I know nothing about Brinley except that she hasn't gotten over her divorce and one day, she'll be the boss of Bailey Timber.

I grab a beer, toe out of my shoes, and sit on the couch, turning on the TV and keeping the volume down to a minimum. Clicking through the channels, I don't find much I want to watch, so I leave it on some *Rambo*-looking show with a lot of guns and knives and camouflage. My mind wanders as it usually does late at night.

Thoughts of being on that helicopter and the rush of jumping into the cold ocean. Adrenaline stirs inside me with the anticipation that I'm one week closer to it.

Her bedroom door creaking open pulls me from my thoughts, and for a moment, I wish I hadn't looked up at her. She's wearing short pajama shorts and a tank top with no bra. Fuck me, this is pure torture.

She offers a little wave. "You got my note?"

"Sorry, was I too loud? I can turn it down."

She shakes her head. "I can't sleep. I heard you come in because I was wide awake."

She sits in the chair and pulls the plaid blanket off the arm and over herself. I thank whoever is up above for small miracles.

"Listen, Brinley—"

She puts up her hands. "Don't."

"I should've had more self-control."

She shakes her head. "We both should have, but me running away like that was just juvenile. I wish I had a better answer, but I was embarrassed. Here you are looking like that. Who runs away from a kiss with you?"

I don't say so, but she's right. I haven't been turned down since high school. "Still, we told one another we wouldn't. I'm happy to move out."

Her blue eyes widen, and for a second, I swear fear flashes in them before it morphs into concern. "Do you want to move out?"

"No, but I'm not going to run you out of your apartment. I'll find something else."

She tilts her head and looks at me long and hard. We both know that's a lie. "We can coexist. I have an idea. As soon as something happens that turns you on, write it down."

I arch a brow. "Write it down?"

"Make it a rule and write it on the board." She smiles as if a marker and whiteboard are powerful enough to deny our libidos.

My first thought is that I should write down that she can't wear those pajamas, but the truth is that I love the spank bank material. I'm not some guy who can't control myself, but I'm going to have to be satisfied with jerking off to thoughts of Brinley since I won't have the real thing. I can't afford to do something that will make her run off again. Especially since I have no idea where to find her.

BRINLEY

The next morning, I wake up to the sound of puking.

I throw off the covers and tiptoe to my door, opening it slightly. Sure enough, it's coming from the bathroom and the door to Van's bedroom is wide open. I peek in and see that other than the sheets being a rumpled mess in the middle of the bed, the room is immaculate. There are no clothes on the floor or decorative items or pictures he may have added, just his wallet and keys on the dresser in a small leather organizer.

Another bout of puking draws my attention to the bathroom door. The toilet flushes, and I scurry to my room, slowly shutting the door with a light click as the bathroom door opens.

"Fuck me," Van's gravelly voice says from the hallway, then his feet hammer on the floor back to the bathroom. The door slams shut, and the puking sound commences.

I sit on the edge of my bed, picking up my phone to call Kenzie. I've yet to talk to her about everything going on here because she recently got engaged and I figure she must be busy. The truth is that since she moved to New York years ago, we're not as tight as we used to be. I tend to turn to my cousins for support since they're here in Lake Starlight. But other than Calista, I've been keeping anything to do with Van Adler to myself.

"It's been weeks since we've talked!" she says by way of answering. "I called you this weekend and you never answered."

"Well, hello," I whisper.

"I'm your best friend and I'm getting the silent treatment. What's up?"

"Remember how I needed a roommate because of Calista?"

"Yeah."

"I found one, but it turned out to be a guy."

"A guy?" she screeches, then there's a muffled voice on the other end. "Sorry, sweetie. Yeah, I'll go to the other room. Hold on, Brin." I hear her shutting some doors, then I hear the traffic of New York City. She must have stepped out onto their balcony. "Sorry, he had a late night with a client and is going in late today. Anyway, you're living with a guy and I just heard about this now?"

I rub the sheet on my bed between my thumb and fore-finger. "Well, I mean... I don't know."

"I bet Calista knew."

And this is kind of why I hadn't told her. She's been so hell-bent on competing with Calista or whichever cousin knows something before her. She was the one who never returned to Lake Starlight after graduating college.

"Come on. That's not fair," I say gently.

"Sorry. It's the wedding planning. Both our moms are up our asses about everything."

"I'm sorry. I could fly out..."

"Oh no you don't, Brinley Kelly. I know your game. You'll come out here just to get away from this guy."

"How do you know that?"

"Because if you're calling me this early in your time zone, it means you've been over and over things on your own and can't figure out what to do. So how hot is he?"

I fall back on the bed and sigh. "Superhot."

"I need more details."

"Short brown hair, muscles bulging everywhere, tattoos peeking out of clothing, rides a motorcycle, and cooks. He cooks for me."

"Are you sure he's not your dad?"

"Kenzie!" I shout before lowering my voice. "That's gross."

"I need to get on BuzzWheel more. Anyone snapped a picture?" she asks hopefully.

I blow out a breath. I should've called Calista. "Yes, the other night at the grocery store, someone did."

"Hold please."

I wait, hearing horns honking, the city alive and moving while it's quiet here in Lake Starlight—except for Van in the bathroom.

"Holy shit!" Thank goodness she's no longer next to her fiancé. "How on earth have you not hit that yet?"

"Kenzie. It's been, like, a week, and I'm all messed up in the head because we almost kissed. Then I fled to Great-Grandma Dori's old place."

She's silent and I hear Van groan again.

"You ran to Northern Lights Retirement Center? This is what I was worried about. I know there are a lot of widows there, but Brin, you have to find a grief group your own age."

I'd laugh if it wasn't so morbid. "No, she has this... It doesn't really matter. Fact is, I've never felt like this before."

I hear rustling on her end, then the sounds of the city are silenced. Guess she's back inside. "What about..."

"God no. That was for sex only."

"And this wouldn't be?" I think she's preparing a pot of coffee now.

"I live with him, so there's the whole getting to know one another thing. What if..."

She sighs. "What if you fall for him? Good! You deserve a bad boy. And look at your dad. He isn't irresponsible just because he rides a motorcycle and has tattoos. You need a rebound guy. Use him."

"It's been four years, Kenzie, there is no more rebound. Anyway, let's get to the reason I called you." I sit up on the edge of the bed.

"Well, if you would've called me when you first brought in a male roommate, I wouldn't need to catch up." A muffled sound comes over the phone and I hear, "Morning, babe. Coffee's almost done. Sorry."

Kenzie isn't really one to apologize unless she did something hugely wrong. Her fun, go-all-the-time personality is why at one point, I thought she'd end up with Easton, but they were like oil and vinegar together. In the end, I thought Lance would be her husband one day and we'd be cousins-in-law and raise our kids next door to one another, but that dream died quick.

"So, he's sick. Throwing up in the bathroom," I say.

"Gross."

"I should help him, right?"

"Like clean up after him?"

"Kenzie!"

"Sorry, um… you're Brinley Kelly, so yeah, you should."

"What does that mean?"

"It means you usually help anyone who needs it, so why are you calling me to see if you should help the poor soul in the bathroom?" She slurps her coffee. "Shit. Careful, babe, it's hot. Want an ice cube?"

I hear his deep voice but can't make out what he's saying. A second later, I hear the ice maker.

"You're right. I would help anyone." I'm only second-guessing it because I'm attracted to him. If it were anyone else, I'd already be helping however I could. "Okay, I'm going." I stand up from the bed.

"Go, Brinley!" she shouts.

"Babe, it's fucking early." That was her fiancé, and at the moment, I am not his biggest fan.

"Thanks, Kenz."

"Call me once in a while." She laughs. "And go get some. You need it badly."

"All right. Bye." I end the call and stare at the phone for a moment.

I love our friendship and how when we talk, it's like no time has passed at all. Though we don't talk or see each other as much as we used to. I sometimes think that she blames me, having invited me to New York to meet her fiancé, but I have responsibilities here to my family and to the business. She could come here, but we all know why she doesn't.

I open the bedroom door as Van leaves the bathroom. His pale skin has a sheen of sweat and he runs into the wall before straightening up.

"Oh jeez. I thought I heard you. Feeling pretty rough, huh?"

He wipes his mouth. "Sorry I woke you. Some servers

got a stomach bug yesterday and I think it just hit me. We all ate at the same dive bar in Greywall one night after work."

He clearly wasn't sitting around the apartment missing me while I was away, but what did I expect?

"What can I get you?" I ask.

He shakes his head and walks by me. "I'm good. I'll just be in bed. I cleaned the toilet and sink, but I'll probably be in and out of there all day." Walking into his room, he shuts the door and a whimper echoes into the hallway.

I stand against the wall and chew the inside of my cheek. It's only a virus and will be out of his system soon. He's right, he's an adult and doesn't need my help. I should go get ready for work. I walk toward my room, shutting the door behind me, but Kenzie's words repeat in my head. "You're Brinley Kelly, you take care of everyone." If I didn't have this attraction to him, I wouldn't think twice about calling in and taking care of him.

With a sigh, I pick up my phone and dial the office, then leave a message telling them I won't be in because of illness. They don't need to know it's not my own. Then I dial my mom, who doesn't answer, and I leave a message.

I throw on a pair of sweatpants and a sweatshirt, toss my hair in a messy ponytail, and head out to the grocery store. I buy chicken soup, Pedialyte, and some ginger ale. I get some ibuprofen, although I think I might have some already. I want to be safe.

I walk in the apartment and find Van on the couch, still looking like death but with a little more color to his cheeks. "Hey." I drop the bags on the dining room table.

"Hi." He sits up and goes to stand but sits back down, holding his head.

"You're dizzy. Sit." I hurriedly put away the groceries

and pour him a glass of Pedialyte with ice, then bring it over to him. "Here, to keep you hydrated."

He puts up his hand and shakes his head. "I'm not taking anything. I haven't thrown up in an hour, so I'm not taking any chances."

"It's this, or I call my aunt, who is a doctor, and she puts an IV in you."

He accepts the drink. I didn't think I was all that scary to be honest.

"How many relatives do you have?" he asks after taking a small sip.

"You don't want to know. You've probably run into most of them."

He huffs. "Even when I was with my mom, it was just me, her, and my stepdad. Neither she nor my stepdad talked with their extended families."

"So, your birthday parties were small. Lucky you. I barely had enough room to invite my friends after all my cousins were added to the list." I pull the blanket over his lap and go back to grab some ibuprofen, then hand him two of the pills.

"Nonexistent parties really. Birthdays weren't a big deal in our house. Except for my stepdad, but it was his excuse to stay out all night."

"Oh." I try my hardest not to sound as though I find that depressing. "Soup. I bought soup to make you too." I walk over to the kitchen.

My phone rings and it's the furnace guy telling me that just like he thought it's going to be at least a few weeks before the part for the furnace comes in. I sigh, knowing I'll have to drag Calista into this, so as soon as I finish on the phone with him, I text Calista to let her know what's going on. I'm just shoving my phone in my pocket when Van calls my name.

I peek my head out of the kitchen.

"Don't you have work today?"

"I took off. You looked really bad this morning and I didn't want you to be alone."

His eyes soften and the slowest, most adorable smile tips the corner of his mouth. "You didn't have to do that."

"I wanted to," I say without mentioning the pep talk from my friend.

"Thank you."

I nod and go back to the kitchen. When I return with his soup, he's asleep with the blanket pulled up to his chin. I stop and stare, admiring him from afar. God, he's gorgeous.

While he's sleeping, I clean up the bathroom and wash his sheets. I feel odd doing that, but he'd clearly sweat through them. Besides, his room is so organized that as long as I don't snoop, I won't find anything he wouldn't want me to.

He's in and out throughout the day but mostly out of it until seven o'clock, when he says he's going to try to take a shower.

"Are you sure you can stand?" I ask.

He laughs, a sign he's feeling better. "If I fall, call 9-1-1."

"Seriously, Van. I can't help you if you hit your head."

His hand touches mine. "I'm fine, honestly. Thank you for today. I owe you a big favor, so name it whenever."

Automatically, the question, *Will you have sex with me to help me get over my dead husband so maybe I can move on?* comes to mind, but I just smile at him. "I'm sure you'd do the same for me."

"Definitely." He winks and the bathroom door clicks shut a moment later.

I throw myself in the chair, my legs flailing like a toddler having a tantrum. Why the hell does he have to be so damn hot? It would make this whole situation a lot easier if I wasn't attracted to him.

twelve

VAN

I'm off today, so as a thank-you for Brinley taking such good care of me the other day when I was sick, I decide to bring her lunch.

But when I pull up to Bailey Timber, I'm reminded it's not some mom-and-pop shop she's being groomed to take over. In fact, there's a gate and a guard before I can even get on the property. And since Brinley doesn't know I'm coming, I'm not sure what's about to happen.

The guard glances my way, and for a second, he looks as if he's just going to open the gate, but then he does a double take. I roll down the window and the crisp fall air enters the car.

"Do you have an appointment?" he asks.

"No. I'm here to see Brinley Kelly."

He cringes as though he wishes I would've said anyone else. "Let me call up there."

We both look toward the big office building that resembles a log cabin, which makes sense given that it's a lumber company.

"Listen, I'm her roommate and she recently did something really nice for me. I'm trying to repay her by surprising her with lunch. If you could let me get in there…"

He holds up his gloved hand. "No can do. If you don't have an appointment, I can't let you up." He steps toward the phone in the booth.

I have no specific reason for him not to call Brinley. If he calls, I'm sure she'll let me up, but I'll have lost the element of surprise. And for whatever reason, I really want to see her reaction when she realizes why I'm here. So, because desperate times call for desperate measures and all that, I blurt out, "Call Savannah Kelly."

He stops middial and looks at his partner. The expression on the guard's face radiates more fear than when I said Brinley.

"Um…"

"Please, just call her. She knows me. Tell her I'm surprising Brinley."

He blows out a breath, looks toward the other guy, who nods, and dials the phone.

Thank fuck.

"Hi, Hope, this is Elias down at the security gate. Could I talk to Mrs. Kelly? Thank you." He puts the phone down under his chin. "She's putting me through."

We both wait and my leg bounces with anxious energy.

"Hello, Mrs. Kelly, this is Elias down at the gate. I have a Van Adler here. He wants to surprise Ms. Kelly with lunch. Since he doesn't have an appoint… are you sure? Okay." He hangs up the phone. "Mrs. Kelly said for you to go inside, and she'll meet you in the lobby to show you the way."

"Thanks, man." I ease my truck past the gate and take the winding road to the building.

I park in a visitor parking spot and grab the bag with our

lunch in it. Walking up to the building feels like the first time I looked over the edge of the helicopter at the choppy waters below. Brinley is going to run this entire company one day. I can't imagine the pressure that accompanies something like that, and that's coming from someone whose main job is to save people's lives in treacherous situations.

I walk into the building and Brinley's mom is leaning against the security desk with a carrot in her hand.

"Well, look who came to visit." She bites the carrot, and I can't help but wonder if it's a subtle hint that if I hurt her daughter, that's what will happen to my dick.

Swallowing hard, I hold out my hand to her. "Nice to see you again. I apologize for interrupting your day, I just really wanted to surprise Brinley myself and not have the guard call her."

The security guy behind the counter slides a pass over and Savannah hands it to me. "Put that on and let me escort you to my daughter."

She shares a look of mischief with the security woman, whose name tag reads Charline.

To my surprise, Savannah puts her arm through mine and escorts me to the small elevator bank of two. "So, this is Bailey Timber." The doors open and we step inside. Once we're alone, she eyes me from across the elevator. "So, tell me... my husband is very worried about you spending time with our daughter. Give me a reason I shouldn't listen to him."

Shit. I should've had the guard call Brinley. "We're not romantically involved. I'm bringing her lunch as a thank-you for taking care of me the other day when I was sick."

Her head rocks back and she crosses her arms. "When she called in sick."

I put up my hands. "I never expected that. I told her to go to work, that I could handle myself."

She waves her perfectly manicured hand. "That's not Brinley, but I have a sense that you scare her."

"Scare her?" I frown.

"Before she was married, she would light up a room." Savannah smiles, but it doesn't reach her eyes. "She had an exuberance for life and to live it fully, but after... it all vanished. Some of it has come back, but she's forcing it. A mother can tell."

The elevator dings and the doors slide open. A woman in her sixties is standing there waiting for us. "She's in the bathroom."

Savannah nods. "Perfect."

She walks me to an office with a big desk that faces two chairs and a couch. Bookcases line one wall and a small chair sits in front of the window looking out at the lumber mill behind the building.

"I'll go now. Don't do anything her dad and I would do in here." She winks and walks toward the door.

"Thank you, Savannah."

"You can repay me by doing more things like this for my little girl." She smiles and shuts the door, and I hear her and the older lady giggling as they walk down the hall.

I walk over to the window and stare out. If I didn't work for the Coast Guard, I'd only be qualified to work in that mill, not in this building. There's no telling where I would've ended up. Brinley and I are on opposite sides of the financial spectrum, that's for sure. Why the hell did she need a roommate?

"Van?" Her voice rings out and I turn. She's standing in the doorway, a smile of surprise on her lips. "What are you doing here?"

I walk over to my bag. "I brought you lunch."

"Oh." Her smile widens and her cheeks pinken.

That's the exact reaction I was hoping for.

TEN MINUTES LATER, we're seated in her office at a small table that overlooks the lumberyard. Her door is shut, and she asks her assistant, Hope, not to disturb us. Oh, the things I would do to her in this office if she were mine.

"I didn't interrupt you from anything?" I ask, taking a piece of fried chicken.

She finishes chewing a forkful of the pasta salad, shaking her head. "No, I'm looking at forecasts for next year and my brain can't handle any more numbers. It's... well, enough about here." She picks up a piece of the fried chicken and bites into it, the juice dripping down her chin. "Oh."

She pulls the chicken away, looking for a napkin, so I wipe her chin with the clean napkin in my hand.

"Thank you." Her eyes cast down to her plate.

"You're welcome. I have to say I'm glad the chicken isn't dry."

She laughs. "Definitely not dry."

"So, tell me more. What's it like to have a family empire?"

We both look out the window at the stacks of lumber, a few workers talking and pointing at different areas of the yard.

"I have no idea how my mom does it. It's been in our family for a long time. After my great-grandpa died, my grandpa took it over, but... you probably don't know this, but my grandparents died in a snowmobile accident, so my mom took over the company when she was pretty young. My great-grandma taught her everything she needed to know."

"I saw the pictures down in the lobby. You'll be up there one day."

She scoffs and moves her pasta salad around her plate with her fork. "I guess."

"You don't like the pasta salad?" I eye her plate.

"Oh no, I love it. It's just talking about taking over this company sort of ruins my appetite. Like, if something happened to my mom, I'm not sure I could step up the way she did. She was built for this and I'm just not sure I am."

"Why do you say that?"

She shrugs. "I think everyone thinks that because I look like my mom, my personality must be like hers too, but I'm not like her."

"How are you different?" I take another bite of my chicken.

She leans back and rests her forearms on the arms of the chair, linking her hands together where they meet in the middle. "I don't know how to explain it. She's in her element here and I don't think I'm in mine, but I made promises and after... I went to school for business and everyone, even Sawyer, thinks this is where I belong."

My eyebrows slam down. "Sawyer... that your ex?"

She glances toward the door. "Yeah."

"Who cares what he thought? Go back to high school before there was any pressure to figure out your whole life. What did you love to do then?"

She laughs. "That's pointless. It doesn't change what I do here."

"Humor me."

She stares out the window for a second and I don't think she's going to answer. "I loved art class."

I nod. "Your dad's a tattoo artist."

She nods. "I never really put that together actually. Are you suggesting I got that from him?"

I shrug. "I don't know, maybe. But what if you take some classes or just draw on your own free time?"

"I'm so busy. I don't know. I answered, so how about you?"

"I was busy trying to survive, going from shelter to shelter when I was in high school. I had no idea where I would end up. I just wanted to get to eighteen, so I couldn't be thrown in the system."

She frowns then bites into a strawberry. "I'm sorry. You don't have to tell me. I know we have our rule regarding talking about the past."

"Maybe it's unrealistic of us to assume we can live together and not talk about this stuff." I bite into my chicken.

"Probably. I find myself curious about your life."

I laugh and she smiles. "It's not that interesting, believe me."

"It's so different than my own. From anyone I know actually."

I put down my chicken and wipe my hands. "Well, I couch surfed at my friends' houses sometimes. Most of their parents worked the night shift, so they didn't know it. But when I turned eighteen, it was time I finally did something. But the thought of making enough money for an apartment with only a high school diploma... I just didn't want to struggle, so I did what a lot of people in my position with few options looking for direction do. I joined the military."

Her eyes widen. "Really?"

I nod. "It kept me housed, clothed, and fed. In a lot of ways, the military was nicer than my mother."

"I can definitely see how you'd end up there. Did you love it?"

"Yeah. I really did." I shrug. "I thrived there and felt a sense of accomplishment. I liked the fact that you got rewarded for your hard work." She can probably hear the yearning in my tone. How much I miss it. I'm counting down the weeks until I'm back on base where I belong.

"Not like here, where the owner's daughter gets the job." She stares out the window again. At times like this, I feel like I lose her to her thoughts.

"I have no doubt you could do this job if you wanted, Brinley, but it's clear this isn't your dream job."

She turns to face me and shakes her head. "But who really gets to live out their dreams? Dreams die every day for millions of people."

"Just like millions of people live out their dreams every day," I counter.

"True, but I'm not one of them." She picks up her fork and takes a few bites of everything I made. "This is really good. Thank you so much for bringing me lunch."

And like the snap of a finger, she changes the subject. Since I'm leaving in a few more weeks anyway, I decide not to push her.

thirteen

Around dinnertime, I'm shutting down for the day when my mom walks into my office.

"I'm just about to leave," I say.

She sits on the couch, slips off her heels, and tucks her legs under her body. "You don't have a few minutes for your mom?"

I stop what I'm doing. That's her guilt trip because when she was my age, her mother had already died. Dad reminds me of that every time Mom and I go head to head with one another.

I walk over to the chair next to her and sit, then extend my legs on the coffee table, crossing them at my ankles. "If this is about Van, I'll remind you again that we're just friends."

"Friends who bring one another lunch and friends who call in sick to take care of each other?" She tilts her head questioningly. She's been on me for years to move on from Sawyer's death.

"Our relationship really is platonic."

"Because you're making it that way or because you're not attracted to him?"

I shrug and pick at my fingernails. This is why I barely paint them. I'm too anxious to have beautiful nails like my mom always does. "Both maybe."

Her head falls back and hits the back of the couch as a huge belly laugh tumbles out of her. "Sweetie, you can say a lot about that man, but unattractive isn't one of them. When I walked him up today, he turned the head of every woman in the office—and a few of the men's too."

"It's because he's huge and has tattoos."

"Yes."

"Mom, he's your type, not mine."

She stares into space. "I know, and if I was younger, I'd snatch up a guy like that."

My face screws up at the thought. "Hate to break it to you, but I've been told the stories about you and Dad getting together. You didn't sound like a willing participant at first."

Not really, but I read Great-Grandma Dori's notes on the mission board. How they had to twist my mom's arm to get her to admit her feelings for my dad. She had way too many hang-ups because he was four years younger and her twin brothers' best friend. But I'm not telling her about the mission boards yet. Maybe ever.

"Everyone is cautious when it comes to the heart. Especially when I had all this on my shoulders to keep our family afloat." She motions around the office. "Everyone was relying on me, and I didn't see where a personal life would fit in. Your dad showed me how that was possible and that I needed him to love me. The lust between us became love and there was no turning back." She gets that soft expression she always does whenever she talks about my dad.

"That's the thing, Mom. I didn't shy away from love and look where it got me."

She blows out a long breath. Concern glints in her eyes. "Brinley, I told your dad the night of Sawyer's funeral how worried I was about you. Up until then, nothing bad ever happened to you. Sure, you grew up without your grandparents, but you had Dori until well after you became an adult. I think, in some ways, that made you think it was a good idea to get married so young. I know you were happy with Sawyer and loved him. I know, sweetie. But I think you thought that you two would live happily ever after and nothing bad would ever happen. You guys bought that ridiculously expensive house without much forethought on what it would take to keep it running or what would happen if the market changed, then it all crashed down around you. And what happened to Sawyer was awful, the worst thing that could happen. But for four years, I've watched you just stand still and not move forward. My biggest fear for you that night has come true, and I wish I could turn it around for you."

I abruptly stand. "Jeez, Mom, you make it sound like I'm damaged goods."

"You're not damaged goods. You just don't believe in anything that can only be felt anymore. If I had a glass ball and saw a future with you and someone else, you'd probably go for that man, but since no one can predict the future, you'd rather stay holed up, alone." She straightens her legs and slides her feet into her heels. "Your dad and I are going out tonight. Want to join us?"

I shake my head. "No, I'm going to go work out and then home, so I can come back for another shift here."

She walks over to me and rests her hands on my shoulders, staring into my eyes. "I love you, sweetie, and I just want you to be happy. Tell me to stay out of your business, and I will."

"Stay out of my business," I say, tilting my head with a smirk.

"I'm sorry." She cringes. "I just can't. You're my baby."

"I thought Asher was your baby."

She shrugs. "He's off at college, hopefully not sowing too many wild oats. I have no interest in being a grandma quite yet." She laughs, her forehead falling against mine. "I love you."

"I love you too, and I'll admit, Van is very attractive. But he's hiding something. I just can't figure out what it is."

She tucks a strand of my hair behind my ear. "Have you told him everything?" Her eyebrows rise.

"No."

"Well then, maybe he senses that you're not being one-hundred-percent open and letting him in. Of course he'll close himself off a little."

"We're roommates," I say, and she laughs again.

"Anyone in the room with you two knows there's much more than shared rent between you." She kisses my forehead. "Now you made me all sappy and yearning for your father, so I gotta go."

"Mom," I groan.

"Oh, grow up, Brin, you know your dad and I have sex." She's at the door, her hand on the knob. "And you should be having sex too. If anything, just for fun." She eyes me over her shoulder and walks out.

I plop into my chair. "Why does everyone have an opinion about my sex life?"

ON MY WAY home from the office, my aunt Cleo calls, so I answer it on Bluetooth.

"Hi, Aunt Cleo."

"Hey, Brin. How are things?"

"Good."

"We're planning a trip down to the ice cave next month. I'll put you on the list."

"Is this the singles thing?" I hit the button on the steering wheel to increase the volume a bit.

She laughs. "Oh, I forgot! Rumor has it you already have someone, huh?"

"Where'd you hear that?" *BuzzWheel, I'm sure.*

"Does it matter? What's he like?"

I shake my head and stop at a stop sign. "He's the exact opposite of anyone I've ever dated. And he's just sharing an apartment with me."

"Opposites are good. Your uncle and I were opposites."

I nod, not in the mood to hear someone else's love story as if that's going to get me over my own. I shift the conversation. "Anyway, what did you need?"

"Oh well, we just got word that the network is having a reunion of the show your uncle and I used to do a long time ago. And it's the same weekend as the camping trip with the twins' Girl Scout troop. Is there any way you could go in our place? We'd owe you big time. The network is paying us too much to pass up the opportunity. I've called almost everyone else, but they're all busy."

I make a turn onto Main Street in downtown Lake Starlight. "All fifty of us are busy but me?"

"Well, you know, it's not like I would send them with

just anyone. Calista can't do it, and you're the one I trust as much as her."

"When is it?" I'm such a sucker for this kind of thing and my entire family knows it.

"This weekend." I can practically hear her cringe.

"Seriously?"

"I know. The network was just kind of hovering and not making a decision, but once they did, we only had a certain window to do it, what with the storm that's supposed to come next week. Denver said it was this weekend or next spring."

I sigh. "Okay, send me the details. When do you leave?"

"Well... that's the other thing."

I groan and wave to my uncle Austin's best friend, Jack, as he comes out of his hardware store, Hammer Time.

"I need them to spend the night at your house on Friday, then the campout is Saturday."

"Okay. I'll grab them after school and take them home with me."

"Oh, Brin, you're a lifesaver. Thank you so much."

"You're welcome."

"Sending details right now." I hear her clicking some keys on a computer, then she says, "Sent."

We say our goodbyes and I eye a parking spot up ahead on the street. I park along the curb in front of the apartment, and as I'm stepping out of my SUV, I spot Van with his hand on the small of a woman's back, escorting her into Uncle Rome's restaurant, Terra and Mare.

What the hell?

The door shuts behind them and I'm almost breathless from surprise. But why am I surprised? We're not involved, and just because he brought me lunch as a thank-you doesn't mean he likes me. Here this entire time,

I thought we were attracted to one another, but he's dating. I shake my head because it's really none of my business.

I go to my apartment door with my key in hand, but as much as I want to push what I just saw out of my head, I can't. My stomach is roiling, and my chest feels tight. Without any forethought, I pull out my cell phone and hit the button to dial Lance. He picks up and I blurt out, "Let's have dinner. Terra and Mare?"

"Um... okay. Sure."

"Great. Hurry up and get here." Then I hang up.

I head back down the stairs and out onto the street to wait by my car. I don't want to walk into the restaurant alone, but then again, it's prime dining hours. If I wait, I might not be able to get a table even if I am the owner's niece. Shit. I text Lance.

Me: Did you leave yet? You better have left.

HE TEXTS BACK RIGHT AWAY.

Lance: Will you relax, I'm on my way.

I PACE the length of my SUV until I spot Lance parking his sports car that I can't believe he hasn't already put away for the season. He snags a spot in front of Terra and Mare, so I walk over there.

"So, what do I owe this impromptu dinner to?" He puts on his suit jacket and straightens the lapels.

I tug him toward the door. "Because you're my cousin and best friend."

We walk in and it's dark, so I don't immediately see which table they're at. Then I spot them in the last table to the far right. Van's in a button-down and slacks and looks delicious.

The hostess knows us, so she sits us at one of the shittier tables by the bar. Not that I blame them. We don't get charged for our meals here, but Uncle Rome told us to make sure we always tip appropriately.

Lance, like the man he was brought up to be, takes my coat and holds out my chair. Just as I'm sliding into the chair, my eyes meet Van's, and he tilts his head. He knows Lance isn't my boyfriend, but at least now he knows I see him. I smile politely at Van and sit.

After Lance tucks me in, he leans down so his mouth is level with my ear. "He's on his way over." Then he goes to the other side of the table.

"Brinley." Van stands at the edge of the table. Up close and personal, he's drop-dead gorgeous. So handsome in fact that I open my mouth, and nothing comes out.

"Hey, Van. Good to see you again," Lance says.

He turns his attention to my cousin, and thankfully that gives me time to collect myself. "Nice to see you too." They shake hands. "You guys should join us."

I shake my head. "We wouldn't want to intrude."

"We haven't even ordered. Please, I insist." He stops a waiter and asks if we can join him at his table.

I know the answer before they give it, so I slide out of my chair and grab my coat from the back of the chair.

Lance's eyebrows rise as we walk over, and Van holds out the chair next to him for me.

"I hope you don't mind. I've asked my roommate and her cousin to join us," Van says.

The dark-haired girl looks familiar, and it isn't until Lance refers to her by name that I remember she works at Lucky's.

"Sabrina, nice to see you." Lance sits down next to her and ignores my glare.

"Hi, Sabrina." I put out my hand. "Brinley Kelly."

"I know." Sabrina shakes my hand limply.

Why did I walk in here in the first place?

BRINLEY

Before anyone has an opportunity to say anything else, the waiter comes over to take our drink order. I order a glass of wine and Van clears his throat. I turn in his direction and he's smiling in an almost condescending way that grates on my nerves.

"What?"

He ignores my challenging stare. "She'll have a beer and so will I."

My head rocks back a bit. "Excuse me?"

"Don't order wine because you feel like you should here. Just have a beer." Van shrugs.

"Maybe I wanted the wine," I snipe.

His head tilts and he raises his eyebrows.

"You know you prefer beer, Brin," Lance chimes in.

"You always get it at Lucky's," Sabrina adds.

I'm about to grab my things and storm away from this table, but instead, I look at the waiter. "I guess the table has spoken. I'll have a beer instead."

"Which one?" the waiter asks.

"She'll have a Blue Moon and I will too," Van says.

My hands squeeze into fists in my lap. "I didn't know you were this bossy."

"Just making sure you have a good time tonight." He winks and faces Sabrina.

She orders wine, then she and Lance decide to split a bottle. I kick him under the table, and he straightens his back, giving me a mean look.

We order our meals too, and thankfully when Lance asks if our uncle Rome is here, we're informed he's not. The last thing I need is him breathing down my neck about what exactly the situation with this foursome is all about. He'd probably say he's out of pasta and can only give us one helping, so we could *Lady and the Tramp* it.

"We're sorry for intruding," I say more to Sabrina because Van took it upon himself to move us over here without asking her.

"It's okay," she says.

"I'm taking her to dinner as a thank-you for taking over my shifts this weekend."

"Oh?" My eyebrows rise into my hairline.

"Yeah, I forgot to tell you that I have to head out of town this weekend, but I'll be back late Sunday."

I look at Sabrina. "He doesn't have to answer to me. We're just roommates."

I don't know why I'm giving her the green light. If I really didn't care if she went for Van, I wouldn't even be sitting here right now.

Lance sparks a conversation with Sabrina about her commuting to the University of Anchorage, and when he finds out she's studying hospitality, his face lights up.

"Lance's family owns Glacier Point," I inform Van.

"Shit. Really? That place is nice. I spent a few nights

there when I first got to town. That's why I had to find a place to rent. Glacier Point is hard on the bank account."

Lance laughs as though he understands the struggle, but it's not like he's ever had to worry about money. The guy is a trust fund kid who will someday take over his family business that makes billions. He has one foot in our town and one in New York, but eventually, he'll have choices to make. "If I'd have known, I would have cut you a deal."

"Especially since he's military," I say.

That piece of information grabs Lance's attention. "You are? We have discounts for veterans. Thank you for your service."

Van nods. "Welcome."

"Are you still in the military?" I ask, remembering I never found out the night we had that conversation.

"No," he answers, but it's clear to me that there's more to the story.

I decide not to get nosy about which branch and where he's located since I'm getting the vibe he doesn't want to discuss it. I'm assuming Anchorage since there are a few bases there, which would make sense since he ended up in Lake Starlight.

"You couldn't miss a better weekend. I have my twin cousins spending the night Friday, then we're doing a camping retreat on Saturday night."

"What?" Lance looks surprised as the waiter arrives with our drinks.

"For the Girl Scouts." I pick up my beer and take a sip.

"How old are they?" Van asks.

"They're ten."

"You're taking them all by yourself?" he asks, looking surprised.

"Yes. I'm fully capable. Born and raised Alaskan here. Plus, I was a Girl Scout a long time ago."

"Oh, I loved the campouts." Sabrina smiles, sipping her wine. "So much fun. If I didn't have to work, I might've asked to go with you."

"I know, me too. Although I worry about getting it all set up okay, once that's done, I'll be fine. Plus, they have other parents, so I won't really be on my own."

"Is it the whole troop going?" Van asks, a crease along his forehead signaling his worry.

"Yeah."

"All women?"

My eyes narrow. "No, dads go too."

Sabrina nods. "Yeah, my dad took me."

"You should go with her," Van says to Lance.

Lance points at himself, eyes wide. Him setting up a tent and eating hot dogs and s'mores?

I laugh. "Yeah, no."

Lance's expression clearly says he wants me to shut the fuck up. "I wish, but I'm in New York this weekend at a charity gala."

"Man, you live the life," Sabrina says.

"It's what a degree in hospitality will get you." He smiles.

"Along with a granddad who already built an empire," I say good-naturedly.

"And I'm so different than you how?" Lance raises one eyebrow.

"I'm not worth billions." I take another sip of my beer.

"Bailey Timber is a big company and could be even bigger if the family hadn't agreed to halt the growth years ago."

I tilt my head at Lance and give him a look that says we

should not be discussing family business in front of other people, but Lance shakes his head and sips his wine.

For the rest of the dinner, we engage in polite conversation. Sabrina is really nice even though I wanted to scratch her eyes out when I saw Van put his hand on the small of her back. I really need to figure out exactly what I feel for him and what I want to do about it.

As I hug Lance while we all say goodbye to one another, I whisper, "Thanks for coming on such short notice."

"That's what cousins slash best friends are supposed to do." He squeezes me tight. "If you need to talk, I'm here day and night."

"I know."

He pulls back and glances at Van walking Sabrina to her car. "Eventually, the day will come though, you know."

My forehead wrinkles. "What?"

"When you'll be too weak to fight."

"Stop being cryptic. What are you saying?"

He looks at Van again, who's now waiting for me to walk to our apartment together. "If it's not him, it'll be someone else. At some point you'll tire of fighting a connection that's clearly there. Sawyer would want you to move on, Brin. It's been long enough. You were clearly jealous tonight. Dig deep and figure out why that was and address it. Don't ignore it and let another four years pass you by."

I throw my arms around him again. "Thanks, cuz."

"One day you'll probably have to get my head out of my ass, so don't worry about it."

We laugh even though that will never be the case with Lance. He's just waiting for the right girl to come along, then he won't wait to snatch her up.

"Not you. Easton, well..."

We laugh again.

"We'll have to double-team him." Lance kisses my forehead. "Now go." He climbs into his sports car.

"You'll have to put that thing in storage soon," I call.

"Tomorrow. One last ride before I go to New York." He runs his hands over the steering wheel. "Bye."

He drives off and I walk over to where Van stands on the sidewalk, looking like the perfect mix of gentleman and bad boy in his suit.

"So?" he says as I approach.

"So what?" I ask.

"You were jealous." He says it like a blanket statement, and I can't help the way it gets my back up.

"Um, no. I was having dinner with my cousin." I walk toward the apartment and he walks alongside me.

"So, you always enter a restaurant and inspect who's in there?"

I balk. "I didn't. Maybe when you eventually saw me, I was glancing around."

"I saw you the second you walked through the door. Hell, I *felt* you. The hairs on the back of my neck rose like they always do when you're near."

My steps falter for a second, but I force myself to continue walking. God, does he realize what it does to my resolve when he says stuff like that?

We reach the building and I walk up the stairs to our apartment. "Whatever."

I get to the door, but he puts his hand over mine. "Stop it."

"What? I was curious, that's all. You're free to date if you want." I insert the key in the lock and push the door open.

Once we're inside, he slams it shut. "Will you please stop?"

"Stop what?" I turn to face him and throw my hands in the air.

He shoves his hands in his pockets. "It must be exhausting."

"Excuse me?"

He brushes by me on the way to the kitchen and glares at me. All the times his gaze has been on me, it's never made me feel like it does now. As though I'm as disgusting as the scum on the bottom of his shoe. I wrap my arms around myself.

He grabs a beer from the fridge and everything inside shakes when he shuts the door. "Pretending to be someone you're not." He leans his hip on the counter, twisting off the beer cap and tossing it in the trash.

"I don't even know what you're talking about."

"I believe the ad you put in the paper said you were really neat and clean."

I say nothing, squeezing my fists at my sides.

"Funny because there's an empty bottle of body wash that's been sitting in the shower ever since I got here." He pushes off the counter. "And how about this? There's a drawer filled with stuff that doesn't go together."

My lips press into a tight line. "It's called a junk drawer. Everyone has one."

He scoffs, feigning shock. "People as neat and organized and put together as Brinley Kelly don't have those."

"Seriously? You're coming after me about a body wash bottle and a junk drawer?"

"I could go on and on. The labels on the cans face every which way. Actually, you don't even put like cans together. Corn is in one cabinet and green beans are in a cabinet on the other side of the kitchen." He opens up the two cupboards as if he needs to show me.

"Sorry if I disgust you."

"Disgust me?" He lets loose a mocking laugh before stopping himself. "I don't give a shit about the empty bottle or the drawer or any of that shit. What I want to know is why you want to be someone you're not?"

Tears gather in my eyes, and I suck in a sharp breath. I cannot cry in front of him. I will not let him see me broken. "I don't owe you anything. I'm sorry if you think I'm pretending, but I have no reason to act like someone I'm not."

I turn to leave the small kitchen, but he stops me, taking my wrist in his hand.

"This is not what I want between us."

I look up at him. "What do you want? Want me to call you out on the weird little secrets you're keeping? That's right, I know there's something you're not telling me. That's obvious enough, given the fact that you don't want to talk about our pasts."

"You were in agreement with that."

"Would it have mattered if I wasn't?"

"None of that matters anyway. You were jealous tonight because you feel this thing between us. I know you do. Admit it, you know there's something more than roommates between us." He releases my wrist to wave a finger between us.

Feeling cornered, I nod. There's no sense denying it. My actions tonight made it obvious.

"Does it help if I tell you I'm scared too?" His voice is soft and sincere.

Suddenly everything Lance said makes sense because I no longer have the strength to deny myself what I want so badly.

I rise on my tiptoes and smash my lips to Van's. He

wraps his strong arms around me, tucking me into his body, and slides his tongue between my lips. In a whirlwind of adrenaline and rapture, now that I'm finally kissing him, all I can think of is him and his tongue as it slides along mine. A million little atomic bursts of energy and pleasure go off in my body. One of his hands slides up and cradles the back of my head as if he's afraid I'm going to pull away too soon.

I slow the kiss and he bends, his lips on my neck and never leaving my skin. "You have no idea how many times I thought of this moment," he says just above a whisper. "When I saw the jealousy in your eyes when you walked in the restaurant, I've never been so fucking happy because I feel the same way you do even after this short amount of time. You're mine and I'm yours. There's no one else in this town that I want." He slides his lips back up to mine and I grip the short hair on his head.

"Why can't you be a horrible kisser?" I murmur along his lips, and he chuckles. Then I remember his words and I strip my lips off his. "Wait. Why would you be scared?"

His shoulders tense and I step back. "Because I have an entire life outside these city limits. A life that's waiting for me, and there's no room for someone by my side."

"Are you married? Have kids? Engaged?"

He chuckles and shakes his head. "No. I'd never ask someone to marry me while I'm enlisted. It's no life for someone else. I'd neglect them and I wouldn't be able to concentrate on my work knowing they depended on me and I was failing them."

His message is so cryptic.

"I only planned on being in Lake Starlight for eight weeks." I open my mouth and he places his finger to my lips. "I wasn't going to leave you high and dry. I'll pay for the year, but I'm only on leave. I'm reenlisting when the eight weeks are up."

It's clear from his facial expression that there's no room for discussion. So I decide to be honest with him. Might as well get all our baggage sprawled open between us and figure out how to clean up the mess after.

"I'm not divorced," I say.

Panic flashes in his eyes. "You're not?"

I shake my head. "I'm a widow."

BRINLEY

"Fuck, Brinley, that explains so much." He pulls me into him. One arm is wrapped around my waist and the other is burying my head into his chest. His natural scent overwhelms me in the best possible way. "I'm so sorry. I shouldn't have said all the shit I did. God, I'm a jackass. Forgive me."

I draw back and our eyes lock. Gathering all my courage, I say, "I'm not just scared, I'm terrified now that I know you're going away so soon and there's really no future for us."

His forehead falls to mine and his hands mold to my hips. "I don't know the answers, but I really like spending time with you. Maybe..."

"Are you suggesting a relationship while you're here and then we stop when it's time for you to leave?" I shake my head because I'm not sure I can do that.

"I'm merely suggesting we don't put a label on it, but I'm also not suggesting we sleep together. If you're not comfortable with that, then we can take it off the table."

I double blink. "Really?"

He shrugs as if ignoring the sexual chemistry between us will be easy. "The only thing I know is I like to be around you. The other thing I know is that you need time. Now that I know you're a widow, I get it. I would never push you into anything."

I wrap my arms around his waist, leaning my head on his chest. "Thank you so much." I draw my head back a little. "I can't promise you anything, Van."

"I know, and it's okay."

I look at him in disbelief. I love that I have no pressure. And maybe it's good that if things go south, he'll be leaving in six weeks to go back into the military.

My phone vibrates in my pocket, and I pull it out to see a text from Lance.

Lance: Thanks for the highlight on BuzzWheel.

I LOOK UP AT VAN. "We made BuzzWheel."

I hurriedly pull up the app. Sure enough, a picture of the four of us at Terra and Mare is front and center. In it, I'm talking to Van, and Lance and Sabrina are talking.

LOOK *who we found at Terra and Mare this evening. A rare foursome. The customers who sent in tips said our newest resident, Van Adler, arrived with Sabrina Thompson. Soon after, Brinley Kelly arrived with her cousin, Lance Whitmore. It didn't take long for Van to usher the cousins over to dine with them, where Lance and Sabrina shared a bottle of wine while Van and*

Brinley seemed to be chatting it up the entire dinner. So, who is dating who? That remains to be seen. The only thing we know for sure is that something is going on with our newest bartender and our Brinley, but I think I speak for the entire town when I say, if you hurt her, Van Adler, we're coming after you.

THEN THERE'S a bunch of comments that say how hot he is, how cute we are as a couple, and how Lance should be asking out Sabrina.

"What's it say?" Van asks.

"Oh, um… it doesn't matter." I push down his hand that's now holding his phone. "Want to veg out for the night?"

"You mean watch *The Mindy Project*?" he asks, one eyebrow quirked.

Thankfully, he's put away his phone. I don't need him thinking people in this town will hurt him if he breaks my heart. They need to know I can stand on my own two feet, but maybe I need to prove it to them first.

"I'm going to change first," I say.

"Great. I'll make some popcorn," he says.

I go into my room and change into my pajamas. As I'm about to leave my bedroom, Kenzie texts me.

Kenzie: Is Lance dating her?

I SHOULD HAVE ASSUMED I'd get a text like this.

Me: Aren't you engaged?

Kenzie: Just answer me Brin.

Me: Did you even read the article, or did you just look at the picture?

Kenzie: The picture says it all.

Me: Lance came with me to the restaurant. She was there with Van. They shared a bottle of wine, so relax.

Kenzie: I am relaxed, I was just curious is all. I mean good for him for moving on.

Me: Anything else?

Kenzie: Don't tell him I was asking.

Me: Never.

THIS HAS BEEN my world since my cousins and I reached puberty. A knock on my door interrupts my texting. I swing the door open.

"You coming?" he asks.

"Yeah, just had to text my friend Kenzie back after she saw the picture on BuzzWheel."

"How come?"

I shrug. "It's just a thing between her and my cousins Lance and Easton."

"Are they involved in a threesome?"

I laugh. "No." I shoo him out of my room, and he brings the popcorn into the living room.

"I'm going to change into sweats. Keep talking." He heads into his bedroom.

All I can think about is him naked in his room and what that might look like.

"Brinley?"

"Oh yeah, sorry." I give my head a shake. "Ever since my cousins got hormones and went through puberty, they've loved the same girl—my best friend, Kenzie. She texted to see if Lance was dating Sabrina. I wanted to tell her yes because she's engaged now, so it shouldn't matter. I don't know if she and Lance still talk or not because I made it clear a long time ago that I don't want to be involved. I shouldn't have answered her questions tonight, but she caught me in a weak moment."

He comes back out into the living room shirtless, wearing only gray sweatpants and, I can tell, no underwear.

"What are you wearing?"

His gaze roams up and down my body. "I could ask you the same."

I look down at myself. "I'm fully dressed."

"Well, turn down the heat and I'll put on a shirt."

"And your boxer briefs?" My eyebrows rise.

He smiles in a way that hits his eyes and lights up his face. It's a smile I haven't seen before and it's contagious. "Then you put panties on."

"How do you know I don't have them on?" My voice is way breathier than I want it to be.

"Because you keep wearing these little shorts-and-shirt sets and I'd bet big money you aren't."

A rush of heat travels through my body. My shorts

aren't fitted, so I know they can gape a bit. "Have you seen it?" I whisper, not sure how I want him to answer.

"What do you want me to say?" His voice is gravelly, and his eyelids look heavy now.

"Okay, rules board." I stomp over to the dry-erase board. "I'm adding another one. No sweatpants without underwear or a shirt."

"Why? I'm comfortable and this is my apartment too." It's the first time I've ever gotten pushback from him, and for some reason, it turns me on more.

"Because I can see the outline of your thingy." I point with the red dry-erase marker toward his groin.

"My cock is not a thingy," he says seriously.

I cover his mouth with my hand. "Don't say that." He bites my palm and I pry my hand off his mouth. "You bit me."

"And I'll bite you in other places I promise you'll love. Stop acting all polite and proper." He steps closer to me. "You'd love it if I ground against your core right now. I'd dry hump you so good you'd fall apart in my hands."

I stare down between us. His dick is half-erect already. I lick my lips then clear my throat. "Do you have to say those things?"

He wraps an arm around my waist. "I told you I'd never ask you to do anything you weren't ready for. If you say no, I'll respect it. But I never said I'd make it easy on you."

I turn in his arms, and he steps up to my back, the bulge in his sweatpants landing on my lower back. When he bends his knees, it pokes me in the ass. His finger runs up my leg but doesn't pass the hem of my pajamas.

I swallow, trying to coat my suddenly dry throat.

"It's on the rule board." I point at where I added it.

He takes the marker from my hand and hovers over my

head. "And you can't wear these pajamas without panties. So we're clear." He leans down to my ear. "I'm only saying that as payback. I really have no problem with you going commando." A shiver runs up my spine and he places his lips right under my ear. "I'll be in the living room."

I compose myself as best I can, drawing in a cleansing breath. "Water?"

"Need some water, do you?" he teases me, but when I glance in the direction of his voice, he's coming from the hallway to our bedrooms, throwing on a T-shirt. "I'll take one."

I grab us both a water and meet him in the living room. He's sitting in the middle of the sofa with the bowl of popcorn on his lap.

"Where will you sit?" The way he says it, I can tell it's a challenge.

I sit down next to him and grab the blanket from the chair to cover my lower half.

He turns on the show and leans in close to me. "Good decision. Popcorn?"

I take a handful and pick up one piece at a time, barely able to concentrate on the show because he's so close. His cologne, his intrinsically male scent, his big hard body— everything is sensory overload. I find myself staring at him more than the television.

"You keep looking at me and we won't be watching this for very long," he says without turning his head from the TV.

"Sorry. It's just... I don't know... it's weird. I haven't done this with anyone since Sawyer."

He turns and stares into my eyes. "Then this is step one. Get used to having someone to cuddle with. I'll keep my hands to myself until you say otherwise." He holds up his hands.

"Why are you being so patient with me?"

"Because you're worth it."

"Van." I sigh. He cannot tell me he's leaving in mere weeks and then say things like that.

"Just have some popcorn, enjoy the laughs, and stop overthinking. We're just two friends watching Netflix. Except for the fact we want to rip each other's clothes off and fuck like bunnies. Just ignore the last part."

I spit out my water from laughing and he shakes his head, handing me a Kleenex from the box on the side table.

We spend the night barely touching except by accident, and when he yawns for the millionth time, I hit Pause and say we'll watch more tomorrow.

I fold up the blanket as he puts the bowl of popcorn in the sink and throws the water bottles in the recycling. On his way back, he locks the apartment door. As he stands in the doorway to the bathroom and I stand in my bedroom doorway, we lock eyes.

The urge to negate the distance and put my lips on his is fierce. But I know exactly what that will lead to, and I don't know if I'm ready yet. I have a feeling that when the two of us do come together, I'm going to need to be ready.

"Thanks," I say.

"Stop thanking me. Good night, Brinley." He steps forward and kisses my cheek.

"Good night."

He disappears into the bathroom, and I walk into my bedroom, shutting the door. I do a double take when I look at my bed because something is on my mattress. I step forward to see it's a sketchbook and pencils with a note.

· · ·

YOU NEVER KNOW *until you try. Draw me something as beautiful as you. ~ Van*

I CLUTCH it to my chest. "Thanks, Van," I shout.

"You're welcome." He's right outside my door, knowing I'd see it and probably wanting to hear my reaction.

God, what am I going to do with this guy? He's not chipping away at my walls, he's bulldozing right through.

sixteen

VAN

The next day, Brinley is at work and my shift at the bar doesn't start until five, so I do my laundry, clean the apartment, and after becoming antsy, I decide to call my commander. I talk to his assistant first, and she forwards me on to him.

"You were on strict orders, Adler," he says by way of greeting.

It's quiet in the background, so I assume he's in his office.

"Just wondering how the weather is in Kodiak, sir."

He laughs. "Bullshit. How are your orders coming?"

I shake my head and sit on the couch. "You mean my orders to find a life that doesn't include the Coast Guard?"

"That would be the one. I issued it myself."

"Which, in truth, isn't really your call. Maybe I want to be married to the Coast Guard."

The conversation is quickly turning into the same one we had when he denied my paperwork to reenlist until I took all the time off I've accumulated. I don't want to go down that same path today.

"Don't make me keep you on desk duty when you get back."

"Sorry, sir. You have to be missing me by now though."

He laughs again. "A hotheaded alpha male who thinks he's the best diver in the guard? I have plenty just like you."

"We both know you don't."

"Is the reason for this call for you to convince me to let you come back early?"

I consider his question. Is it? I'm not really ready to come back, but that's only because of Brinley. After last night... I don't know. I feel compelled to see what could happen between us.

"I know we have a meeting scheduled this weekend."

"Adler, you don't need to come see me. When I said check in, I meant a call like this one. Jesus, you'll do anything to get back on base." He blows out a breath. "You need to find a life. Ever since..." He blows out a breath. "You haven't taken any leave like you should, and you're hyper-focused on what's going on here to the point that you seem almost obsessive about your job. It's not healthy. You need some perspective. You'll be a better member of the service if you take this time and use it wisely."

He'd know, I suppose. He has a wife, three kids, and a house. On the rare occasions I've seen them all as a family unit, it looks nice, but I learned a long time ago that you can't always trust how a marriage looks from the outside. My mom would smile and be nice during my stepdad's work functions, but she was always on pins and needles that she didn't set him off. Otherwise she might see the back of his hand once they got home.

"Yes, sir. I'm trying. But about this weekend, some-thing's come up and I—"

"I hope it's your dick that came up. Except I'm not sure

you ever had that problem while you were on base. Is it a girl?"

"In a way, but not the way you're thinking."

I can imagine his shit-eating grin as he doubts that what I'm telling him is the truth.

"Listen, I got more important shit to do than to talk to you all day. I don't need another check-in. You report back after your eight weeks are up and the paperwork will be ready for you to sign. Remember what I said, Adler, you got one life. One life and that's it. It's way too short to spend it all with us. Plus, we're getting sick of seeing your ugly mug. Have a good leave, Adler." He hangs up.

I stare at the phone for a moment before tossing it on the couch next to me.

One thing is for sure—if I'm going camping this weekend with Brinley and her cousins, I'd better get us equipment. I'm sure Brinley thinks she has everything under control, but I have a little expertise at stuff like this.

I jot down a small list. If I was in Kodiak, I'd just go to my storage locker, but that's not feasible, so it looks like I'm spending my day shopping.

I'M SHOCKED when at about seven o'clock, Brinley walks into Lucky's by herself. I'm clearing a couple glasses off the bar from a couple that just left, and I signal her over. Her dress is tight at her small waist, but it wraps around her body, so there's a dip at her cleavage. It's professional but still sexy as hell. I'm secretly jealous of every one of her coworkers for getting to admire her in it all day.

"You meeting someone here?" I ask.

She gives me that smile as if I'm trying to pull information out of her. "No, long day at work and I was bored at home, so I figured I'd come here and have a drink."

"Well then, what can I get you?"

She smiles again and it's as though we have our own secret language because she doesn't even have to say the words. A rush of energy settles in my stomach.

"One beer, coming right up," I say.

Sunrise Bay is expecting a storm, so Lucky's isn't busy, which means I get to spend a little extra time chatting with her. She drinks her beer and eats the pretzels from a new bag I opened just for her as we watch the television.

"So... this Girl Scout thing..."

Her eyebrows furrow. "What about it?"

"It's mostly dads, right?"

She laughs then sobers when I don't. When she leans over the bar, I shamelessly glance at her cleavage. "You can't be jealous. We're taking baby steps here, remember?"

"Weren't you jealous of my dinner with a coworker last night?"

"No," she scoffs, but she loses her serious expression a second later. "These are married dads, and I don't go after married men."

"I bet they aren't all married. Some are probably divorced or maybe never married in the first place."

"I wouldn't know since it's my cousins' troop. Other than helping them sell cookies, I don't get background checks on the parents." She sips her beer.

I raise my hand and say goodbye to a group of four who say they need to get home before the snow gets too bad.

"I should go." She slides off the stool.

The only people left are a twosome over by the pool tables and they're just finishing their drinks.

I cover Brinley's hand with mine. "Wait. I'll walk with you after I get off."

She hesitates and glances at the couple in the corner like I did.

"You don't want to leave me all alone, do you?" I give her a pleading look.

"All right, one more."

I get the bottle out and screw off the cap, putting it in front of her. "I'll be right back."

I toss her old bottle in the recycling and head over to the couple by the pool table. They're pretty intimate and a jealous feeling settles in my stomach. Why do I want that so much? Because I want a night with Brinley. A night where I can kiss her and undress her and discover all the noises she'll make as I settle on top and inside of her.

"Can I get you anything else?" I ask the couple.

The guy downs his drink and looks at the woman he's with, asking her silently if she wants another round.

"We need to get home." She finishes her drink, and the guy hands me his credit card.

I ring them up and return it to him.

After they've left and I'm cleaning off their table, I whistle toward Brinley, whose attention is on the TV.

"Want to play some pool?" I ask.

"Aren't you working?" she asks, but she's already sliding off her stool and bringing her beer and pretzels with her.

"There's no one for me to serve and we're closing early tonight because of the storm. I've got an hour to kill. Humor me and keep me busy?"

"You don't know what you're in for, Adler." She picks up a pool stick and chalks it.

"I'm in the military. Hate to break it to you, beautiful, but I live at bars with pool tables."

She laughs and sips her beer. "I come from a family of serious competitors."

"Then let's wager." I rack the balls before grabbing my own stick.

"All right."

"What do you want?" I ask, and her gaze tracks down my body. "Whatever you want, Brinley," I say in a low voice.

She bites her lip. "Well, I need to sketch someone, so if I win, I get to sketch you."

"Done. And if I win, I get to take you on a date in public."

"Fine, but practice your poses because you're about to lose."

"Big talk. Break 'em."

With complete confidence, she makes her way around the pool table and lines up her stick, resting it under her finger. The stick slides back and forth a few times, then her gaze rises to meet mine as she draws the stick back and pushes it forward. It goes right between the first and second rows, sending the balls flying. A solid goes into the right corner pocket.

"Guess I'm solids."

I wave toward the pool table and she lines up her next shot. She sinks two more balls and misses the third by a hair when it bounces out of the pocket.

I come up behind her and lean down to say into her ear, "My turn now."

She doesn't say anything, but her body shudders to my lips being so close. She shudders and her eyes close for the briefest of seconds.

I line the stick up for my shot, and the ball sinks into the middle left pocket.

"Show-off." She tips her beer to her lips.

"That's nothing. Enjoy the view."

I position my next shot, and although I have an easy ball right down the right side of the table, I purposely pick a trickier shot just to tease her. I bend forward right in front of her and hit the ball so it banks off one side and into the pocket on the other side. When I stand, her eyes are still where my ass was.

She rolls her eyes and shakes her head. "We don't need to talk between every shot," she says when I open my mouth.

With a grin, I line up my next shot. Although it should be an easy one to knock in, I somehow misjudge the dimensions and it bounces out of the pocket the same way it did to her.

"Oh, my turn so fast?" She jumps off the barstool and gets some chalk, running it down the length of the stick with both her hands.

I clear my throat and adjust my stance to make room for the half chub that's now between my legs.

"You okay, Van? Something in your throat?" Her hands run up and down the length of the pool stick.

"You play dirty." My voice is gravelly with need.

She smiles and slides by me. "Excuse me."

Her breast brushes my chest, and my hand reaches out to stop her by the hip, but at the last minute, I remember she isn't mine yet and I let my hand fall back to my side. She sets up her shot, bending forward in her dress. Fuck, I wanna slide my stick up the back of her dress so I can see her panties. I bite my lip.

She continues to run the table. I get one last chance at

victory, but when I get to the eight ball, I miss the shot by a millimeter, setting her up with a perfect shot.

"What pose will you do for me, I wonder?" She stares at me while hitting the ball in.

"You beat me. Let's go two out of three." My cell phone interrupts us, and I step away to answer it. "Hey, Nate. Yeah, last couple left about a half hour ago. Thanks." I hang up. "We're closing even earlier than expected, miss. You'll have to take your hustle somewhere else."

She laughs. "Oh, you assumed I couldn't play because I'm a girl?" She puts her stick back and I cage her against the wall while I put mine back.

"I would've posed regardless," I say.

"And I would've gone on a date."

For a moment, we stay there, my lips an inch away from the bare skin that I want to taste so badly. But I pull myself away, knowing she needs space. I'll have to be happy with flirting for tonight.

"Come on, I'll take you home," I say, picking up her beer bottle and bowl of pretzels.

As the snow falls, the two of us don't hurry back to our apartment, and when she almost slips in her heels, I grab her hand and don't let go the entire walk.

If she minds, she doesn't say anything. Thank God because it feels better than I thought it would. That should scare me, but for some reason, it doesn't.

The girls are eating their breakfast in front of the television because I'm their cousin, not their mother, when Van walks out of his room in those damn gray sweatpants with no shirt. At least he has underwear on this time because there's no outline.

He stands in the doorway and rubs his eyes. He had a late shift last night, so the girls and I didn't see him before we all went to bed in my room. He looks at them with a confused expression as though he woke up in the wrong apartment.

The twins stare at him, then each other, then back at him.

"Who are you?" Abby, the more direct twin, asks.

I laugh and pause while packing up our s'mores stuff. "This is my roommate, Van. Van, these are my cousins, Abby and Allie. We're going camping tonight, remember?"

He nods and winks at them. God, can he ever stop flirting? "Hey, girls. I'll be right back."

He heads into his bedroom and comes back out while putting on a shirt. I love watching his muscles constrict as he slides the fabric over his body. I miss the view of his chest the minute it's covered. What must it feel like to slide your hands down the planes of his chest...

He walks over to where I am near the door and inspects the bags I set on the floor. "All you have are s'mores and hot dog buns? These sleeping bags are light, they're not going to keep you warm." I bite my lip as he practically pushes me aside to get a better look at everything I packed. "Where's the tent?"

"Already in my car."

He nods. "Flashlights? Extra batteries?" He leans closer to me. "Tell me you have a gun and knife?"

"Well, um..."

"Shit, Brinley." He lightly grabs my arm and drags me into the kitchen. "You're not prepared." I open my mouth to respond, but he keeps talking. "This is why I'm going to go with you."

I let my hip cock out. "Does this have to do with the dads again?"

"No, but I can't believe they don't send out a list of necessities and stuff. I'll hop in the shower."

"We have to get going in a minute."

"Where is it?"

I shake my head. "Van, honestly, I think you've—"

"Where is it, Brinley?"

"The high school."

"I'll grab my truck and supplies and meet you there. We'll leave your car and take my truck for obvious reasons." He walks away, mumbling to himself about how *we live in Alaska, there's damn snow on the ground, and how irresponsible it is to camp in the first place.* He stops in front of the girls. "I'm going to meet you over at the school. Don't let Brinley leave without me."

Abby crosses her heart. "Promise."

"Girls," I say, urging them to tell him he's worrying over nothing.

"Thank goodness you're coming because we were a little worried ourselves," Abby continues as Allie nods her head.

My god, these little plotters.

"No worries, I'm in the military and I'm trained for this kind of thing. I've been in much worse situations than what's out there now."

Allie and Abby smile as he walks into his bedroom.

"Why didn't you tell him it's an indoor campout?" I whisper-shout.

"Because he looks like fun. Plus, everyone always has their dads. We need a man there." Abby picks up her cereal bowl and brings it to the kitchen.

"We do not need a man there."

"If anything, he's eye candy," Allie says.

My jaw hangs open. "Allie!"

She doesn't say anything and follows her sister to the sink. They rinse their bowls and set them on the counter.

"You're taking after your dad," I say. "Go grab your coats and stuff."

I walk to my bedroom as Van walks out of his room. "Just a quick shower and I'm right behind you."

"I need to tell you something before you spend your entire Saturday..." Then I recall how Sabrina is working for him this weekend because he is supposed to be going out of town. "Wait, you're supposed to be out of town."

"Plans changed, but I'm still off, so I'm coming. Quit trying to stop me because I'm coming no matter what."

He's so persistent that I finally just give up the fight. "Okay then. See you over there."

He smiles, and as usual, I get that fuzzy feeling in my chest. I smile back and go into my room while he goes to take a shower.

Shortly after, the girls help me downstairs with all of our stuff and I announce that we're going to stop for a few more snacks. Sure, they love me then.

We don't need Van. He's going to be so surprised when he shows up though. Hopefully he doesn't get too embarrassed when he finds out this is an inside campout.

WE'RE in the parking lot of the high school and I'm talking to one of the dads, Drew, who I admit has flirted with me on occasion. He's about ten years older than me and divorced for almost six years. He's an attractive man who loves running marathons and is a doctor up in Anchorage, but he wanted his daughter to have a small-town upbringing, so he lives here in Lake Starlight. His daughter's mom still lives in Anchorage, but she rarely sees their daughter even on her visitation days. I have a lot of questions surrounding her, but unlike a lot of my family, I keep them to myself since it's none of my business.

Van's big black truck pulls into the parking lot, and the twins get all giddy, whispering to Drew's daughter, Penelope.

"Who's this?" Drew asks.

"Oh, it's a friend who really wanted to come with us. But—"

I have no time to finish my sentence because Van comes out of the truck wearing jeans, a camouflage jacket, a hat, boots, and gloves.

"Hi, Van."

He walks over, scowling at Drew. "Hey." Van kisses me on the cheek.

I'm sure my cheeks go pink because I feel them heat.

"Glad I made it. I had to make a run to the hardware store for an axe," he says.

"An axe?" Drew says and looks at me. "What on earth are you going to do with an axe?"

Van looks at Drew as though he's an idiot. "Cut down firewood, kindling. We won't survive without fire."

Drew looks at me and I look back at Van. "If you'll excuse us for a minute." I hook my arm in Van's and lead him over to his truck.

A lot of eyes are on us and I'm not sure whether it's because Van looks the part of the hot outdoor survival master or if it's that the two of us are talking. Maybe a mixture of the two.

"So... remember when I was trying to tell you something this morning and you thought I was objecting to you coming, so you kept interrupting me?"

"No." He looks dead serious.

I would've had to cover his mouth with my hand to get him to stop talking, he was so appalled after he checked out our gear.

"Okay, well anyway, we're just camping in the high school gym. The girls get a badge for it and it's just for fun. I wanted to tell you that so you wouldn't feel like you had to come. Feel free to leave." I put my hand on the forearm of his jacket.

He stares at my hand for a second then sets his gaze on mine. "Do you want me to leave?" He shakes his head. "Of course you do. I've embarrassed you, coming in here talking about an axe and making a fire." He looks down at himself and laughs. "Shit, I can't help but laugh at this."

I'm glad he finds the humor in it, but I step closer to his line of vision. "You'd never embarrass me. And I think it's sweet the way you wanted to go with me and the girls to make sure nothing happened to us." And that's the truth.

I don't like comparing Sawyer to Van, but this would not have been Sawyer's thing. He probably would've said I was a pushover and needed to tell my aunt no in the first place. He wasn't a bad guy, he just wasn't family oriented. He liked it being him and me, and how could I ever blame him for that?

"We still have tents to put up. Would you like to stay?" I ask softly, hoping he'll say yes.

He shrugs. "Well, I don't have anything else to do."

I link my hand with Van's. I don't even know why, it just feels right. "Then stay. The girls would love it." I pull him toward the group and stop in front of Drew. "Drew, this is Van. Van, this is Drew."

Drew looks at our entwined hands. I'm not sure what it means, probably another baby step toward what I don't know, but I really like the idea of Van being here with me.

Abby rushes over. "Everyone is putting their tents together. We're gonna be stuck by the bathrooms."

"Hell no, not on my watch." Van releases my hand to go to his truck but stops a few feet away. "I'll watch the language."

I smile and nod. "Come on, girls, let's get our stuff from my vehicle."

Drew and Penelope go to their car, and we all make our way into the gym. We find a spot in the middle of the gym right beside the wall, thank goodness.

"I'll set up a single for myself," Van says.

Besides his company, another good thing about having

Van here is we get all the supplies inside in fewer trips and he takes care of all the heavy stuff.

Once we're ready to go, I open my tent as Van opens his. I practically blink and his is already together while I'm still reading the directions on mine. Abby and Allie are holding sticks and becoming frustrated with my instructions because they're right, they suck. And although I want to show them I'm as tough as their mom, I know Denver does a lot when they go on excursions.

"Do you mind?" Van's hand is out for the instructions.

"At this point, no." I hand them to him, and he glances over them.

"Abby, you put it through that hole, and Allie, go to the other side and get it when it slides through." He directs the girls rather than taking over and doing it himself like I expect him to.

They listen and follow his instructions, and when the pole gets stuck, they all laugh. My heart aches from watching them interact because it's not like there's a future for Van and me, but I can tell that one day, he'll make a great dad. After they're finished, he high-fives them and pretends they hurt his hand.

"Excuse me, Drew," a woman approaches him where he's working on getting his tent up next to us. "Could you help us with our tent when you're done?"

I recognize the woman, but I don't know her very well.

"Sure, I'm almost done with ours and then I'll be over," Drew says.

"I can do it. I see you're still a ways from finishing yours." Van walks over to the woman.

Drew doesn't say anything, but his facial expression is telling Van to fuck off.

"I told you, I have it handled," a man says to his wife when she asks to be next.

I come out of our tent after helping the girls arrange their sleeping bags and see Van halfway across the room, helping someone else put their tent together. Drew rushes over to another mom who has asked for help.

"What are they doing?" Abby asks me.

I watch Van slide in right before Drew reaches her and starts to put it together. Drew shakes his head until someone else asks for help, then he rushes off in that direction.

"You girls are witnessing two men competing to be the alpha male."

"Like lions?" Allie asks.

"Who are they trying to impress?" Abby asks.

"Jeez, Abby, Aunt Brin, of course. They both like her." Allie smiles at me.

I run my hand down her long dark-blonde hair. "I don't know about that."

Then we all laugh as both men scramble to help the next person and they end up on the floor from tripping over another tent that was in the way.

Being wanted does make me feel good, there's no denying that. But if I had to pick a winner, it'd be Van. But he'll be gone soon enough and then where does that leave me?

eighteen

VAN

Once everyone's tents are up, I go back to Brinley and the twins. Brinley is smirking at me.

"What?"

"Sure was eager to help all those families."

I shrug. "What can I say? I'm a helper." I take off my sweatshirt since I layered up, thinking we'd be outside. After the sweatshirt is off, I notice Brinley's gaze on me. "I have another layer I'm taking off."

"Maybe you shouldn't. I mean, I'm not sure I can keep them all at bay." She laughs.

It strikes me that I've never seen her so carefree. I'm so happy she's showing me this side of her. I grab my thin, long-sleeve shirt and pull it up over my head.

"And there're all those eyes. It's like a Chippendale dancer just came into the room. Oh wait, some of the parents are going to their purses for dollar bills. You better put that back on."

I bend down and tickle her rib cage and Brinley howls with laughter. "Who told you?"

"We did!" Abby and Allie say in unison, smiling like traitors.

"Let me go. Seriously." Brinley squirms and wiggles.

I eventually let her go so we don't make too big a scene.

"I'm hot too," Drew says next to us and takes off his sweater, leaving him in a gray T-shirt and not looking nearly as impressive as me. He's fit but looks like he might have a runner's body. While I don't want to be conceited, I'm bigger and I'm built.

"I picked a shirt that was snug to keep the body heat in." I run my palm over the shirt that's clinging to my chest and Brinley looks back at me again.

"Yeah, I would've too if we were going outside." Drew gives me a grin that doesn't reach his eyes.

Who is this douche? I was obviously talking to Brinley. First, he competes with me on the tent thing, and now he's setting up shop right next to us.

I sit down and stretch out next to Brinley, propping my head up with my hand. "I hope it's not embarrassing for you?"

"Are we talking about your shirt?"

I nod.

"Um... are you kidding me? I feel like I have what everyone wants. The women and the men."

I chuckle. "So, what do we do at these things?"

"We make s'mores, and I have a big surprise this year," Drew chimes in again, sitting with his knees up and his arms wrapped around his legs.

"A surprise, huh?" Brinley asks.

It better not be for just Brinley.

"The girls are going to love it. Penelope knows, but I swore her to secrecy."

"Cute," Brinley says with a smile.

"Do we play games? Something to keep them occupied?" I ask.

"They keep each other occupied," Drew says.

"They do have activities, but I swear they're the same ones every year. At least that's how it was when I was a kid."

I frown. "Ghost stories?" I ask Brinley.

"They're ten," Drew answers for her.

"Okay, buzzkill." I sit up, not about to lie around all day and watch ten-year-olds play together as though we're conducting a psych thesis. I turn back to Brinley, who's staring at me and probably wondering what my game plan is.

"Let's play some games. Maybe we can do a scavenger hunt? This is a high school. There has to be a lot to do."

Brinley nods as though she's game but doesn't know what exactly to plan. I rack my brain for what could be a fun game.

"Capture the flag," I suggest.

"Everything is locked up in the PE closets. They don't allow us to use the stuff." Drew is really getting on my nerves.

"Okay, give me a few. Brinley, why don't you split everyone up into four teams? And make sure I'm on your team."

I leave the gym and head out to my truck. I grab some old T-shirts from my bag and scour the area for branches. Once I have enough stuff, I go back inside, tear the shirts apart, and tie them on the sticks.

Soon I've garnered the attention of the Girl Scouts, who sit in front of me and watch. Some of their parents stand behind them, while Brinley's to my left, giving me that look like I'm showing off.

"It's like when the Hulk used to rip his shirt open," a grandma who is here with her granddaughter says.

"That's if he was tearing off his own shirt," someone corrects her, but my gaze travels to Brinley, who is shaking her head after obviously hearing it.

I get the flags made with the help of a few dads who aren't intimidated by me.

"There's an auxiliary gym that was open for overflow, so we can play there," Brinley says.

We all walk down to the gym, and it doesn't surprise me that Drew is practically sulking. He must have had high hopes about what would happen between him and Brinley today.

Not on my watch, asshole.

We split into four groups, Brinley and Drew both being captains of opposing teams. I position the flags in the four corners of the room.

"Once your flags are gone, you lose," I announce. "Any protection must be ten feet away from your flags."

Everyone agrees, so we all congregate toward the middle of the four quadrants. The captains pick their teams. I tell Allie and Abby to say go when everyone is ready and the game starts. Some of these families are stealthy, but soon it's just us and Drew's team.

We take a five-minute time-out for the teams to talk strategy. We're huddled together, and I give them my suggestion with the hopes it helps and everyone agrees it's the best plan. Getting the flag back to our side will be difficult, but I think it's worth the risk.

I ask one dad to stay back with our girls and the flags. Brinley hops on my back and we cross the line, easily getting past the girls, but Drew is guarding the one flag left. If we grab it and get over the line, we win.

Drew's screaming to the girls on his team, instructing them, and when I dodge left, he blocks. I dodge right, and he blocks again. Then I run, turn my body right toward him, and Brinley hops off my back.

Drew is so concerned with me that he tags me, and I laugh as Brinley grabs the flag and runs toward the line. He realizes too late, but a mom jumps in Brinley's way. Brinley shuffles her feet and the mom comes after her, but Brinley does this spin move and jumps over the line into our territory.

"We win!" I shout, probably a little more ecstatic than I should be for a Girl Scouts game.

"Jesus, no one invited you," Drew snipes.

I pat him on the back. "Don't be a sore loser. It's not a good example for the girls."

Brinley runs toward me and jumps into my arms, her legs wrapping around my waist. My dick is like, "hell yeah," but there's nowhere but her ass for me to put my hands, and this is a G-rated event.

I release her reluctantly, and she rises on her tiptoes and kisses my cheek. "That was the best. Oh, the adrenaline rush. What a great idea."

The twins run over, and they each hug her, then me. "This is so much fun. What's next? What's next?" They're jumping up and down with wide eyes and big smiles.

The leader of the troop comes over and shakes my hand. "Thank you, Mr. Adler, that was fun, and the kids definitely enjoyed themselves. I think everyone must've worked up an appetite, so we're going to get the pots going in the cafeteria to boil the hot dogs."

I look at Brinley. As if she can read my mind, she gives me a look asking me to let it go. "Boil? You don't put them over a fire?"

The leader, who is probably in her thirties with her hair pulled back in a very sleek ponytail and her shirt buttoned all the way to her neckline and tucked into a pair of jeans, is clearly a rule follower. I should quit while I'm ahead.

"Well, this is an inside campout. The girls understand," she says.

I nod, not wanting to ruffle too many feathers. "And what about the s'mores?"

"We use marshmallow cream." She says it proudly, and I wonder if she can hear herself.

"I could build a fire pretty quick." I try to keep my voice casual, as if it's just an idea.

She waves off the suggestion. "Oh, no. We're on school grounds."

"There's the spot a little farther out where students build bonfires," Brinley suggests gently. "I could run to the store and get some skewers for the girls."

The leader thinks about it for a moment, then smiles. "Sure, let's do it. It isn't too cold out and the girls all have their coats. Those who get cold can come back in. Boy, we sure are getting a treat having you here, Mr. Adler."

I can't fight my smile. "Thanks."

I miss doing all this stuff. When I first came to Kodiak, I'd take my leave every year and go camping or just travel to different places with my tent and live off the land. I loved it, but that changed a while ago. Maybe my commander is right. I need a fucking life. I keep thinking he means marriage and kids, but maybe this is what he means. Not have all my focus on my job and trying to get better at it to mitigate risk. Maybe that isn't healthy.

Brinley's going to the store, so I recruit some dads to help build the fire. Even some of the girls join us, grabbing kindling. We're a large group, so we need it to be pretty big.

An hour later, every girl has a hot dog on her skewer and her parents are helping her cook it over the fire. The twins each have one and I take turns helping them.

Brinley is across the fire, talking to a mom. Our eyes catch over the flames, and I can't tear mine away. She's so beautiful. The first time I saw her, I felt this pull in my heart, but I thought she already had someone. It wasn't that long ago, but in some ways, it seems like a lifetime ago, as though I've known her far longer than I have.

Maybe we're both too messed up to pursue anything. I mean, she's a widow and needs extra care from the obviously traumatic loss of her husband, and I still harbor ill feelings toward marriage. Beyond that, I don't see how I could be in a serious relationship with anyone once I reenlist. I give everything I have to my job, which doesn't leave much for anyone else.

The girls love the hot dogs off the fire and some of them go back for seconds. Adults put out the other snacks they brought. Families sit together on the logs that the high schoolers must've put here for their bonfires.

"Now s'mores!" the leader shouts. "I'm told that Penelope's dad has a big surprise for you all."

Brinley glances at me, and I roll my eyes.

"Instead of Hershey's bars, we've got peanut butter cups!" Drew holds up the orange package.

"Oh boy." Brinley sighs.

"What?" Drew says, forehead creased.

"Don't open that!" a woman screams from the far side of the fire.

"Relax, Ana, I have this," the leader says to the screamer. "Drew, I think you may have forgotten, but we can't have peanut butter due to allergies."

"Oh, right." Drew's shoulders sink.

I feel bad for the guy. He really thought this was his moment to shine. I'm half tempted to console him, but Brinley is beelining right for him.

Well, fuck. Here I've been trying to impress her all afternoon and all it takes to get more of her attention is failure?

She talks to him for a few minutes, and they share a laugh that makes my jaw clench. I understand exactly how Brinley felt when she saw me with Sabrina and I don't like it one bit.

nineteen

After the girls are asleep, I sneak outside to visit Van, where he's waiting for the fire to go out completely. It's down to embers with a few flames, but it's calming fast. I'm sure Van knows how to put it out properly if he wants to come inside, so I'm curious why he's out here.

"Hey, you," I say quietly, trying not to startle him, but his body still jolts where he stands close to the fire, long stick in hand.

"Hey."

"Did I spook you?" I step up so I'm shoulder to shoulder with him.

"Nah, not at all." He looks down at me, his smirk saying he's lying.

"Thanks for today. You made it a whole lot more fun for the girls."

He chuckles and puts down the stick he's poking the fire with. "Come sit with me. There're no prying eyes here." He sits on a log and I sit on his lap, putting my arms around his neck. "I wish things were different, Brinley. I wish I wasn't leaving next month. I wish I was one of those guys who hated the military and wanted out, but it's the only place I've ever really seen my worth."

So, this is what he's out here thinking about. I run my hand over his five-o'clock shadow. It's prickly, and it's hard not to wonder what it would feel like on my skin if he was kissing all over my body. I'm pretty sure this is the conversation where he tells me he's noticed all the looks I've given him today and how it changes nothing. He wants to make sure I don't have any expectations that will cause me to be hurt, and I respect that.

"I think it's ridiculous that you only see your worth through your job, but you don't have to worry about me. I don't have us halfway down the aisle because you can keep a Girl Scout troop enthralled for an afternoon. Although it is very impressive."

The flame ignites enough to light up his face and allow me to see his smile at my compliment. I think maybe he doesn't have a lot of people in his life who tell him how great he is.

"I never want to hurt you. So far, this town has welcomed me, you especially, and I'd hate myself if I left you hurting more than when I arrived." His hand lifts my jacket and shirt, his fingers running a figure eight on the side of my stomach. "But that doesn't mean my attraction to you isn't at a point that I struggle to contain myself at times. If the flirting bothers you—"

"No. I like it. Probably too much. I've been up at night a lot lately, thinking about what I want to do with you."

He waggles his eyebrows. "Mutual, babe. Mutual."

I chuckle. "I mean, if I want to cross that line, if I'm ready, and... well, only a few people know what I'm about to tell you."

"Brin…" His voice makes it clear he's giving me an out.

"I want to." I rest my head on his shoulder and stare into the fire. This will be so much easier if I don't look at him. "About a year after Sawyer died, everyone was on me about moving on and how I couldn't mourn him forever. How I was so young, and he would want me to move on. Yada, yada, something I'm sure all young widows hear. So one night, I went to a bar in Anchorage where no one would know me. I dressed to pick up a guy and hung out at the bar all night." His body stiffens under me, but I continue, wanting him to understand why this is such a hard line for me to cross. "A guy approached me, offered to buy me a drink."

"Brinley, is this gonna make me want to go find someone and kick his ass?"

"No, I promise, but thank you for the offer." I kiss his stubbly cheek and rest my head back down where his lips land on my forehead. "So, we spend a couple hours laughing, listening to the live band. I purposely don't drink a lot, and from what I saw, he was nursing his drink as well. At the time, I thought I couldn't ask for a better guy."

I swallow down the embarrassment of what comes next because if Van and I are going to cross that line at some point, he needs to be aware of what might happen.

He's quiet and patient and doesn't rush me.

"At the end of the night, he asked if I wanted to go back to his place. I followed him in my car because I didn't want to be stranded. I never went off the pill after Sawyer passed away and I brought a box of condoms just in case. He drove to a nice house on the water. Come to find out, he was there on business and his company put him up there. I thought it was perfect—I could sleep with him and never see him again."

"But no?" His deep voice rumbles in his chest.

I shake my head against his chest. "No. We talked, and I barely drank the drink he fixed me because I was so nervous. I went to the bathroom and looked at myself in the mirror and told myself I could do this. But I was far from ready. I'd been comparing him to Sawyer the entire night. But when I opened the bathroom door, he was standing against the wall and he held out his hand and asked if I wanted to join him upstairs. I accepted."

His hand tightens on my hip, and his jaw clenches where it rests on top of my head.

"I'm sorry, maybe—"

"No, continue." His voice comes out hoarse.

"We went upstairs, and he was really gentle with me, wasn't urgent in any way. He slowly undressed me and took off his own clothes because I was so in my head about everything that was going on. I told him I had condoms, and he laughed, saying he could take care of that. He disappeared into the closet and came out with a brand-new box, meaning he came on the business trip intending to hook up with someone. Or I don't know, maybe he was just hopeful." My eyes burn from tears that will flood out when I say the next part.

"Hey, there's no judging here," Van says. "I can't imagine what it was like for you. Only you can. Don't feel like you have to finish."

I sit up but continue to stare at the fire. "He hovered over me and did some foreplay to try to get me into it, but I think he could tell I wasn't reciprocating. I just froze trying to keep my distress to myself because there was so much guilt building up inside me because I thought I shouldn't enjoy it. Sawyer was dead, and there I was, naked with another man. I lay there the entire time reprimanding myself for disrespecting my husband." I wipe the tears falling down my cheeks. "Finally, he put on the condom and just as he was about to enter me, a strangled cry ripped out of me, and he backed off, sitting back on his ankles. I lay there naked and told him the entire story. How I just wanted to get it over with. He tried to get me to relax, drew me a bath, but nothing worked. Eventually I apologized profusely, got dressed, and raced out of there." Shame and embarrassment flood my body, and my cheeks heat despite the chilly night air.

Van pulls me into him, kissing the top of my head and resting his lips there. "I'm sorry, Brinley. I can't imagine."

I draw back and place my hands on his cheeks. "I don't know what's going to happen, is what I'm saying. I'm really attracted to you, and I want you so bad. But what if..."

He shakes his head. "We're taking this slow, and I'm fine with that pace. If it doesn't happen, it's fine."

"What I'm saying is that I *want* it to be you. I want you to be my first after him."

He inhales a big breath and lets it go.

"I'm not saying take me on this log. I'm just saying that before you leave, I want us to share being together because, under normal circumstances, we probably would've already. And all I want is to be normal." My voice cracks on the last sentence.

His eyes glue to mine as if he's thinking about it.

I've never had chemistry like I do with him, not even with Sawyer, though I would never tell another soul that part. With Van coming into this town and making me laugh, *really* laugh for the first time since Sawyer's death, I can't help but feel as if he was sent here just for me. And if we can't have a happily ever after, I at least always want to remember him as the man who pulled me out of my grief and helped me move on from the past.

He tucks some hair behind my ear. "Okay, but we're going to take it slow."

I nod. "No time frame. Just—"

"I know." He inches forward but stops himself. "Is this okay?"

"Yes."

He presses his lips to mine, but he doesn't slide his tongue into my mouth. It's just his soft lips against mine until he pulls away. "Thank you for trusting me."

"You're welcome. It feels kind of like losing my second virginity." His eyes go wide, and I laugh. "Relax. I'm just kidding." Kind of.

"Come on. It's time to get you to bed." He urges me up and stands with me, then pours some water on the coals and moves them around with the stick to make sure there aren't any hot spots before taking my hand.

Inside the quiet gym, right before he slides into his tent and I slide in with the girls, he whispers, "Brinley?"

"Yeah?" I say, inching closer to him.

"I'm going to miss you."

I smile, sort of a sad one, and press my lips to his. When I lean back, I whisper, "Me too."

Then we each crawl into our tents and the girls swarm me, making the tent feel so hot it's like I'm going to suffocate. I don't get much sleep, my mind whirling about Van and how much I care for him already.

I can't believe I told him that story. Recalling it still feels mortifying, but he's trustworthy and he has to know if I plan on trying to cross that line with him eventually.

THE NEXT DAY, as I'm driving the girls back to their parents, Abby and Allie are arguing in the back seat over who's going to marry Van.

"Girls, he's almost twenty years older than you."

Abby looks at me through the rearview mirror. "Fine. Then you marry him." Her expression is one I've seen on Uncle Denver before—like she's issuing a challenge.

I shake my head. "Not going to happen. I'm sure there will be boys like Van when you get older."

"Do you think he'll come to the Girl Scout outing next year?" Allie asks, voice filled with hope.

How do I explain to ten-year-olds? Answer: I don't. It's a conversation for next year, though they probably won't even remember him. I have a feeling I'm the only one who will remember Van Adler after he leaves Lake Starlight and I kind of like that. He'll always have a piece of me, and I'll have a piece of him.

"Why are you smiling?" Abby asks.

"Nothing."

"We know you like him. You guys were staring at each other over pancakes this morning," Allie says.

"You know he's a better cook than you, right?" Abby asks.

I balk, but they don't care.

"Not to hurt your feelings," Allie adds.

"I know. Whatever he put in those pancakes was good."

The three of us chuckle.

"Dad prides himself on his. I won't tell him Van's beat his any day of the week," Allie says.

Abby, on the other hand, will probably tell Uncle Denver exactly that, then I'll get the phone call about it. They're right though, so now I need two things from Van before he leaves—his pancake recipe and a passionate night of raw, animalistic sex. I don't think that's asking too much.

I laugh at my thoughts and Abby looks at me through the mirror as though I'm crazy. I can't deny I haven't been myself since Van crossed over the Lake Starlight city line, but I'm starting to think that might be a good thing.

VAN

It's been more than a week since my conversation with Brinley by the campfire. The idea that she wants me to be the first man she's been with since the death of her husband… talk about some pressure. But the thought of going back to Kodiak without having her is unbearable. She's the first woman in a long time I could see myself getting serious with if we didn't live so far apart. Not to mention, I was vague when I said I was in the military. If she finds out I'm a diver with the Coast Guard, I have to think that someone who lost her husband at such a young age isn't going to want to get into a relationship with someone who works such a dangerous job. There's a whole slew of requirements she'll probably have for a future husband, and I can't blame her.

I just want to make sure that whatever happens is on her terms. Every night I've thought about how we'll do this. Should it be our last night together or earlier than that, so there's more opportunity to sleep together before I leave? Then again, she never mentioned sleeping with me more than once. All I know is that it has to be when we're in one of those sexual-tension-filled moments when the energy is hot and undeniable, so she's not in her head.

So, I call Bailey Timber and ask to speak to Brinley's mom, informing the receptionist that it's Van Adler.

"Van," Savannah greets me. "If it isn't our little Buzz-Wheel celebrity. That was quite the article."

After the Girl Scout event at the high school gym, pictures were posted of Brinley and me out by the fire, but there was no accompanying article.

"It was."

"May I ask if you're the reason my daughter's smiling these days?"

I softly say, "I hope so."

"Well, I gotta be straight with you then. It's just too early to ask for her hand in marriage, and you have to ask her father for permission. I know he's a little rough around the edges, but he's a good guy, believe me."

"Oh... no." I stammer over my words. "I-I wasn't calling for that."

She laughs. "I'm kidding. You do know I was young once too?"

"Yes, ma'am."

"Do not call me ma'am."

"Mrs. Kelly."

"No."

"Savannah."

"There you go. So, to what do I owe the pleasure of this phone call?"

"I was wondering if you could give Brinley the day off on Wednesday. It's my day off, and I was planning on going snowmobiling."

"Snowmobiling?" There's a hitch to her voice.

Then I remember Brinley's grandparents died in a

snowmobile accident. Jesus, I'm a moron. I swallow hard. "Yes."

She blows out a breath. "Well, I'm not a very big fan of those machines, but Brinley has ridden them with her father in the past."

"I'm sorry, Brinley told me about your parents. I should've thought of it and planned something else." I feel like a total asshole now.

"It's okay, Van. Honestly, life goes on and tons of people ride snowmobiles every year, and nothing happens. Why not ask her to take the day off? She makes her own schedule."

"I thought about that, but I really want to make it a surprise for her. And I know she's learning to take the company over, and I figured maybe you could push her to take the day off. I'll surprise her in the morning."

There's silence on the other end and I assume she's going to say no when she says, "I like you. My husband doesn't, but I do." Her tone suggests she's smiling. "Done. I'll make sure she's up for anything on Wednesday."

"Thank you so much, ma... Mrs.... Savannah."

She laughs so loudly I pull the phone away from my ear. "Oh, Van, you'll get the hang of it once I'm your mother-in-law. I'm going to go read that new BuzzWheel article again. Bye-bye."

New article? She hangs up before I have time to say anything else.

I hang up and pull up the BuzzWheel app to see what she's talking about.

BUZZWHEEL

Looks like our very own Brinley Kelly has definitely found something with the new boy in town!

But it wasn't only Brinley singing Mr. Van Adler's praises. News hit us that the annual Girl Scouts camping trip at the high school wouldn't have been nearly as fun without Mr. Adler. Not only did he help put up the majority of people's tents, but he put together a capture the flag game, making the flags himself out of T-shirts and branches. Yes, ladies, I'm fanning myself too. Then he built a fire to roast hot dogs and marshmallows. If bartending doesn't work out for him, I think there's an opening to lead a troop and I don't think I'm the only one who wouldn't mind Van Adler sticking around Lake Starlight. He's the epitome of what we're all about and embodies all the qualities we love.

What do you say, Van Adler? I'm pretty sure Brinley agrees.

UNDER THE ARTICLE are a bunch of comments from a lot of the people who were there, some of whom even attached pictures of me with the girls. The only negative comment is from someone who posted anonymously that I didn't put up *all* the tents. Thanks a lot, Drew.

But I've never had praise like that before. Sure, my commanders and superiors are complimentary about my performance and families usually gush after I've helped save their loved one, but I didn't save someone's life this past weekend. I just put together a fun afternoon and these people act like I'm a local hero.

After reading the article again, I do my research to make sure that what I want to do with Brinley is actually happening. I go out to grab a few things we'll need since I want it to be a surprise and don't want to give her a list of things to pack. This is if she agrees to go with me at all.

Once I'm all done, I arrive home just after five. I'm

supposed to be at work at six, so I go to toss every-thing in my room and hear something coming from Brinley's bedroom. It's a sound I would not expect to come out of there unless I was on the other side of the door with her, so I tiptoe over and put my ear to the door.

"Oh, god," her breathy voice says. A long, strangled moan falls out of her, and I lean in closer. "Right there. I knew you'd know my body."

My hand whips to the doorknob, practically strangling it. Why the hell would she tell me all that stuff if she was planning on having someone else?

Anger and jealousy simmer in my blood.

"Come on, harder," she says, and I lose it.

I knock on the door. "Brinley!" There's a scrambling sound, and I rattle the doorknob. "Who's in there with you?"

"Oh my god, Van." She opens the door, and I barrel in past her like a madman.

"Where is he?" I look in her closet and under her bed like some psychotic jealous lover. She can sleep with whomever she wants. It's none of my business.

"I'm in here by myself." Her cheeks are as red as a strawberry in June.

I bite my lip and look down at her. Her pants are unbuttoned and unzipped, revealing a pair of panties I'd love to sink my teeth into.

Holy shit. She was masturbating.

The thought is enough to get me hard in an instant.

She notices her pants are still undone and quickly fastens them up, cheeks bright pink.

"Sorry to act like a caveman, but I can't listen to you making sex noises. I'm going to add it to the rule board." I walk out of her room and over to the board. "No masturbation."

"Are you seriously going to abide by that rule?" she asks from behind me.

I cringe, but she's right. "I am. It's a ridiculous pursuit anyway because it's a waste of my time. I only want you, and my hand doesn't come close to satisfying."

She shakes her head with a cheeky grin. "Well, I've taught myself how to get off pretty nicely in the years since Sawyer died. I'm a little worried you won't be able to compete."

My nostrils flare. "Oh, why don't you show me? It could help me know what you like and be a small step toward the next stage of our relationship." I grab her hand and pull her into me. She fits so perfectly, her head landing right under my chin. "You have no idea how badly I'm going to ruin you. Those toys and your fingers are gonna seem like amateurs once I'm done with you."

And other men, I don't say. I lean against the wall and hold her hips with my hands.

"I hope you do. Now, I think you're due at work soon." She pokes my chest. "And guess what? My mom is kicking me out of the office on Wednesday. Something about my office needing to be checked for pest control?"

"Then you're coming with me on Wednesday. It's my day off, so I'm taking you on a date of sorts."

She squints her eyes. "Do you not remember that I won the pool game? You've yet to pose for me."

"How about when I get home tonight?"

"I'll be in bed."

"Touching yourself?"

She giggles. "*Not* touching myself."

"Cross your heart?"

She brings up her right hand and crosses her heart.

"Maybe we'll have time Wednesday, and if not, whichever day I have off next, I'm all yours. I never asked though, is this naked sketching? Because if it is, I need to do some primping."

"Primping?" Her eyebrows rise.

"Yes, to bring him out in all his glory."

She laughs, and her forehead falls to my chest. "You're something else."

"I'm hard is what I am. If you sketch me right now, you're going to see my hard-on."

"Maybe I want to see it." I move my hands to unzip my pants, but she places hers over mine, stopping me. "Later."

Then I bring her hands up to my nose and inhale. Her scent is as good as I thought it would be, and I close my eyes as if I can relish it forever. I take one of her fingers and put it in my mouth, and she arches it over my tongue. Damn, she's something.

"You taste perfect. Now I'm really going to struggle with this rule." I tap the marker against the whiteboard.

She laughs and walks away. "I'm gonna go change into those pajamas you love so much."

"Rule number two!" I call after her.

"You won't even be home."

I never should've tasted her because I'm more obsessed than ever over what it'll be like to sleep with her. I haven't wanted a woman this badly ever in my life.

I go to work that night only thinking of Brinley and her smell and her taste and her noises. It's a surprise that I make it through my shift without racing back to the apartment, but I struggle through.

When I get home, she's asleep on the sofa. I pick her up

and take her into her bedroom where she startles awake, her eyes bulging out.

"What are you doing?" Her voice is raspy, and it makes me wonder if this is what she'd sound like if I woke up beside her one morning.

"I'm putting you in bed."

"Oh." She relaxes against the mattress. "Thank you. I fell asleep. I put some dinner in the fridge for you. Nothing special, but this way, you don't have to cook before you sleep. I just hope I don't give you food poisoning."

I kiss her forehead. "Go to bed, Brinley. Sweet dreams."

"Night night." She rolls over on her side, and I get a peek of her ass from her pajama shorts riding up. As if I needed that after earlier tonight.

I go into the fridge and see that she made a chicken breast with rice and broccoli on the side. I'm not sure I've ever witnessed her cook a full meal like this. Usually, it's mac and cheese, or sometimes when I'd come home, she'd be eating a bowl of cereal.

My chest warms at the thought of her doing this for me. I've never experienced anyone cooking for me except for the odd girlfriend who never lasted longer than a few months or so.

I heat up the plate in the microwave and turn on the television. I'm almost done with my meal when her door creaks open, and she stands at the entry to the living room, squinting at the lights.

"What's wrong?" I ask.

She shakes her head and crawls next to me, pulling the blanket over her and resting her head in my lap. "I don't want to be alone right now. Do you mind?"

I put my plate on the end table and run my hand

through her hair. "'Course not," I answer, and my voice cracks.

If she notices, she doesn't say anything, but damn, this is intimate.

I turn off the light, my hand running over her side in circles. Eventually, my eyes fail me, and I end up falling asleep right along with her.

twenty-one

BRINLEY

I wake up to the flicker of some infomercial playing. The rock-hard thigh under my ear doesn't move as I slowly rise. Van's head rests on the back cushion, his mouth partly open and his eyes shut. I take a moment to unapologetically gawk at him. He's not the kind of man I'd usually be attracted to. Sure, the muscles and the chiseled chin are hot, but I always picked the safe guys.

I haven't really compared him to Sawyer too much in my mind, which is probably because Van's so opposite. It would just be a list of differences and no similarities, except for the fact that they both give me that feeling of safety, but in very different ways.

With Sawyer, I felt like long term, we'd be okay financially. He worked at an investment brokerage, and even though he was young, he was driven and was already building up his clientele. Whereas with Van, I feel physically safe. Whether it's an animal or a person wishing to harm us, he'd protect me to the death. He's so ruggedly masculine it's impossible not to feel like he can handle anything that comes his way.

And then, on the Girl Scouts camping trip, I saw a side of him I wasn't sure existed. A community man. Everyone loved him. Even BuzzWheel reported on it, and all the parents chimed in in the comments about how much more fun the event was with Van there. The leader asked me if he could help plan next year's campout.

His body stiffens and his head moves right then left before an agonized cry whimpers out of him. He's having a nightmare.

"Van." I grab his hand, but he slides it out of mine.

"No. No," he murmurs. "Go back. I can do it."

His words are almost inaudible, but his body's movements make it clear he's having a nightmare, so I straddle his lap, putting my hands on his cheeks. "Van."

"Just go back," he says, sounding defeated. "Please."

"Van."

I run the back of my hand down the side of his face, and his eyes slowly peel open. He looks around the room as if to figure out where he is and sighs when his eyes meet mine.

"What are you doing?" he asks, blinking as if I'm a vision.

"You were having a nightmare."

"I was? Sorry."

I smile. "You don't have to apologize. Are you okay now? Do you want to talk about it?"

He shakes his head. "No." His hands land on my hips and I rock them on instinct.

Our eyes lock, our faces only lit by the muted television.

"Brinley," he says, and my name sounds like a plea from his lips.

I move my hips again, and his fingers dig into my hips in an attempt to stop me.

"I want to." I press my lips to his jawline, casting a line of kisses up to his ear. "Please, Van."

He breathes heavily, and I feel his body give up the fight underneath me. His hands slide up under my shirt, and his calloused fingertips feel like heaven as they venture along my bare skin. I inch closer to him, feeling his hard length at my core and I'm desperate for more.

"Oh, god," I whisper and rock against it, remembering what I've missed all these years.

There have been times I've craved a man, but being here with him now, I truly mourn the years I pleasured myself because with every little cant of my hips, his dick pulses, and he groans from the pleasure we're sharing.

"Your skin is like silk," he whispers, and his mouth casts open kisses along my neck.

"You're so hard." I run my hands up his torso, the grooves of his abs dipping and rising under my fingertips.

He tears his shirt off from behind his head, and I hungrily admire him.

"How on earth do you look like this?" My hands run down his sides and come to a large, jagged line on his skin. "What's this?"

"Nothing." He slides his hands down my body and his finger dips under the waistband of my pajama pants. "Scar from a fight."

"Oh." I run my hand over it again. I wonder if he ever got stitches for it.

All the questions erase from my mind when he rocks me back and slides his palm down farther, cupping my mound. I must make a noise because he chuckles, then he hooks one of his fingers and teases my clit. I say his name like a prayer to never stop. It's been way too long.

"Take off your shirt. I want to see you," he whispers, drawing back from kissing my collarbone.

With a deep breath, I take the hem of my shirt and pull it off. He stares without apology, then uses his free hand to bring me forward. He takes my nipple into his mouth, sucking and licking and twirling with his tongue. I rock against the heel of his hand, desperate for relief.

He allows it for a second until his hand slides farther down, and he pushes a finger inside me. "You have no idea how long I've wanted to feel how wet I could make you."

"And?"

"You're soaked." He groans and pushes another finger inside. I rise off his hips for a second before growing accustomed to the stretch. "And tight. So fucking tight."

I lean forward, my orgasm rushing too fast, so I slide my hips back and unbutton his jeans and slowly drag the zipper down over his bulge. I get up for a moment, and he helps me by wiggling to get his jeans down to his ankles. He's hard, stretching his boxer briefs, and I glide my hand down his stomach, running my palm over his bulge before pulling down the waistband to rest under his balls.

I stare at his dick and look back up at him. He smirks as if he knows he's big. Bigger than I've ever had, and my insides flex, desperate to know what it will feel like to have him inside me. I go back to straddling him and take the full weight of him in my hands, pumping slowly while my thumb spreads his precum around the tip.

"Kiss me," I tell him, and he brings our lips together, sliding his tongue into my mouth. Then he pulls back a bit and rests his forehead on mine, watching me pump him up and down. He pushes his hand back between my legs. "Your hand feels so fucking good."

"You too."

"Good."

He takes turns moving one finger, then two fingers in and out of me, his palm brushing hard against my clit. My body hums with pleasure, and I clench down because I'm not ready to come yet. I want to make this last. He thrusts both fingers in, and I bolt forward, my head resting in the crook of his neck, my breasts pressed against his firm chest.

He kisses my forehead and I inhale his scent, relishing in the feel of his strong arms. This connection is what a vibrator doesn't do for you.

I tighten my grip on his dick, and a cry escapes him.

"Fuck, don't stop. I'm so close." The desperate quality of his voice ratchets my need even higher.

My hips grind onto his hand and his fingers don't stop, arching to hit my G-spot. He has me right where I want to be, on the cusp of falling, but I want to get him there too, so I clench the walls of my pussy around his fingers.

"I can't wait until it's my dick inside you."

I pump him faster, and he lifts his ass off the couch. Everything around us fades, and I kiss his neck.

"I can't hold it any longer," I say.

"Come apart for me," he whispers and grows thicker in my hand, his hips rising in short bursts as though he's fucking my hand. "Come on, baby, come all over my fingers. Soak 'em."

And at his words, my orgasm rips through me, and I cry out into his throat, jerking in his lap. He stills for a moment and his dick twitches as cum squirts out and drips down my hand.

My head lies on his shoulder while we catch our breath. "Thank you."

He chuckles. "Thank *you*." I draw back and we both slide our hands out, sticky and wet. He takes his two fingers and sucks them clean. "Fuck. Next time my head will be between those thighs."

All I can think in that moment is how I did it. I messed around and I didn't cry. Didn't think of Sawyer and thoroughly enjoyed myself. It feels like progress, like some part of the weight that has been pushing down on my shoulders since Sawyer's death has lifted a little.

He inches forward. "Relax," he whispers before pressing his lips to mine for a chaste kiss. "We're still on your timeline."

I stand. "Shower?"

He smiles. "I'd love to."

I'm not sure where we'll go from here, but I like these baby steps so far.

He turns on the shower as I rinse off my hand and undress, tossing my soaked pajama bottoms on the floor while he takes off his boxer briefs and folds them up with the wet stain inside, then sets them on the counter.

Tension fills the room the same as the steam of the shower as we stand five feet apart, fully naked for the first time. His body is one of an Adonis, pure muscle with trimmed pubic hair and his long thick cock pointed up again, balls tight. He's ready for round two, and I'm still mentally adjusting to round one.

His gaze travels the length of my body. "You're so beautiful. Stunning really."

I push away the feeling of wanting to cover myself up from his examination. He holds out his hand to me and leads me into the shower, putting me under the warm spray of the water first, tipping my head back as his chest rests against mine. The light sprinkle of hair on his chest pokes my nipples and they tighten.

I hold on to his side and again coast my fingers over the raised scar. "Does this have to do with the nightmare?" I turn us around so that he gets under the warm water.

"No." He shakes his head.

"Oh. I just assumed."

He takes my shampoo and squirts it in his hand before putting it in my hair. I close my eyes at the sensation of his fingers on my scalp. Pure relaxation.

"This scar was the final straw that made me move out of my mom's house."

"Your stepdad?" I frown.

"Uh-huh."

"Is that why you never got stitches?"

"He was really going at my mom one night, all because she went out with her friends and didn't have dinner ready for him when he got home. He was supposed to be out, but his event got canceled, and my mom didn't know. He got angrier and angrier that night. My mom's cell phone must've died because she didn't answer when he called. When she got home, she wasn't even in the door two seconds before he backhanded her. I was bigger than him, so I'd made a decision the month before that the next time he hit her, I wasn't going to let it happen again."

He stops talking and turns us around, tipping my head back so the water falls down my hair, rinsing away the shampoo. "I shouldn't have pried."

"Please, you've trusted me with so much. It's not an uncommon story—I got in the middle, and my mom begged me to leave, but I started hitting him, pummeling him to the floor. He called out to my mom to give him his knife."

My heart sinks to the depths of my stomach. Please tell me no.

"At first I was startled she did, you know. That she'd give a man a weapon to harm me, her son, when I was defending her. But I shouldn't have been surprised. Her loyalty had been to him for years. We both got to our feet, and he jabbed out with his knife. Thankfully he didn't plunge it inside me. Ended up being more of a flesh wound."

I bend down and kiss his scar from top to bottom. "I'm sorry, Van," I say, rising on my tiptoes to kiss his lips.

"It was a long time ago." He says that, but I can see the pain in his eyes. I know better than anyone that years can pass and life goes on, but it doesn't mean the pain ever completely disappears.

"You have all these beautiful tattoos. Why not cover it up with something? My dad does things like that all the time."

He puts his hand on his side. "It's a reminder."

"Of?"

He looks at me for a long beat before I see the reason in his eyes. This is why he joined the military—to find his worth because his mother didn't see it in him.

"You don't need that to prove how far you've come. You should get it covered so that you can see another memory, a happier one, when you look at it. Because you're a wonderful man, Van, and what happened wasn't under your control." I hug him tightly, and he wraps his arms around me.

"Okay, let's get this shower over with before we become prunes." He hands me the conditioner, ending the conversation.

With how patient he's been with me, the least I can do is give him the space he needs.

So we shower and kiss and hold one another until we do become prunes. Afterward, with towels wrapped around us, we say good night at my bedroom door. As I slide into a cold, empty bed, I realize that for the first time in a long time, I wish someone other than Sawyer was there with me.

twenty-two

VAN

I knock on Brinley's bedroom door on Wednesday morning and hear a groan from the other side.

"Come on. Date is starting in five minutes," I call.

"Open the door," she says. I turn the doorknob and find her sitting up in bed. "Why so early?"

"It's not early. You'd already be at work at this point."

"I like sleeping in when I don't have to be up early for work though."

I shake my head and hold out the bag of clothes I bought for her, even though I'm sure she has winter clothes. "This is for you." I walk in and place the bag on her bed.

"You bought me clothes to wear?" Her big smile is all the thanks I need.

"I wanted to make sure you were prepared."

She holds her arms out for a hug, and I bend down, wrapping my arms around her small frame.

"Thank you," she murmurs into my neck.

"You're welcome. Now come on because we're going out for breakfast first."

"Oh, where?" she asks, still not getting out of bed.

"How about this? If you don't stop asking questions and get out of bed, I'm stripping down and joining you."

She grins. "Is that supposed to be a bad thing?"

I shake my head and chuckle. "You'd miss the amazing day I have planned for us."

"Very true. Okay." She shoos me and gets out of bed wearing a nightshirt that barely covers her ass.

"Brinley," I groan, sighing.

"What?" She looks at me all innocent-like, but she knows exactly what she's doing.

"Now I have a fucking hard-on." I adjust my dick. "I'm turning on the shower for you."

She mumbles something I can't hear, but I leave the room to wait for her.

She emerges in the living room a half hour later, completely done up.

"I should've told you that you didn't need makeup."

She frowns. "Why?"

"The clothes weren't a hint?"

"You're taking me somewhere cold, that's clear."

"Exactly, but you can put on all the outerwear after we eat. Come on."

We leave the apartment and head downstairs to my truck, where she sees the snowmobile I'm towing.

"You okay with this?" I ask.

"Yeah, I've ridden before with my dad. Some of my family members don't like them, but I think it's different for me. I never knew my grandparents, so I don't have vivid memories of losing them to a snowmobile accident." She gets into the passenger seat of the truck.

We drive to Winterberry Falls because someone at the

bar last week told me about an amazing breakfast and lunch diner that just opened up there.

"Wildberry," Brinley says, reading the sign outside.

We walk in and the atmosphere is cute and relaxed with a French café vibe. We see pancakes, waffles, and French toast being served with whipped cream and a lot of berries. Even one with chocolate sauce.

"Oh, man." She points at one. "Oh, but…" She points at another one a waitress carries past us.

We're seated in a booth and even though I want to sit next to her, I slide in across from her. The waitress comes over and we both order coffee. She asks if we've ever been there before and tells us the story of the two sisters with sweet tooths who own the place. They believe breakfast is supposed to be sugary, but they do savory as well.

Instead of looking at the menu, Brinley seems to be deciding what she'll have by looking at people's plates as they come out of the kitchen. She points at a huge Belgium waffle with whipped cream on top. "That's the one."

"Perfect," the waitress says.

We talk about our week thus far without mention of the other night. Our relationship is like a game of red light, green light. Brinley gives the green, and we go, but as soon as she says red, we stall for a while. But I don't want to rush her or make her feel as if I'm pressuring her. And I have to say, getting to know her better, while kind of foreign for me, is actually really nice.

"Tell me what we're doing today." She sips her coffee, her eyes on me over the rim of her mug that says, "Blow me I'm hot."

"Well, you know we're going snowmobiling, but I'm not telling you anything else." I put a packet of sugar in my cup and stir it.

Brinley points at the cup and laughs. I twist it around and see that it says, "Coffee because it's too early for whiskey."

We both look around and sure enough, there are white mugs with black writing on every table, each one with a unique saying.

"I want to order another cup just to see what she'll give me," Brinley says with a smile.

This is definitely going to be a go-to place for us... then I remember I'll be gone in a few weeks. I make a mental note to bring her here one more time before I leave and swallow down the lump in my throat.

We eat our breakfast, which she only finishes half of because she gets a stomachache. I finish all my eggs and bacon and toast and make fun of her because she should've gone with my breakfast.

Thanking our waitress, I pay the bill even though Brinley argues with me about paying half, and we walk out of the café, seeing the crazy display of cakes and pies in the retro spinning display.

"We should get a cake from here sometime," she says.

"When's your birthday?" I ask, wishing I could take the question back because, in all likelihood, I won't be here for it.

"Oh, um... it's not until next year now. It's a ways off." She waves it off as if it doesn't matter. "Along with Easton and Lance. Did I ever tell you the reason we're so close is that we're known as the Bailey Triplets, all born within a day of each other?" She rolls her eyes. I can't even imagine what it must be like to know someone from day one of your life. "When is yours?"

And there it is. I could easily lie. "Um... we have to get going."

Can't there be something to distract us right now? Her phone ringing, my phone ringing? But there's nothing, and even after getting into the truck, she doesn't fasten her seat belt but stares at me, waiting for the answer.

I blow out a breath. "If I tell you and am honest because I don't want to lie, you can't do anything."

Her face slowly transforms, her lips turning up in a big smile. "It's soon?"

"Next Friday."

Her eyes widen and she claps. "We have to do something."

"Not necessary." I shake my head.

"Not even just one of those cakes and me?"

I wrap my hand around the back of her head and pull her toward my lips, sliding my tongue into her mouth because the thought of her naked and me smearing chocolate frosting and licking it off her body makes me want her so badly. I close the kiss but keep our heads together. "I'll take that."

"Then it's a date."

"I might have to work," I say.

"There's always after."

"Perfect."

I kiss her one more time, a quick peck, before buckling my seat belt and starting the truck.

We get to the park closer to Anchorage to ride the snowmobile since, after our ride, I have something else planned. We both dress in our snow pants and jackets, hats, gloves, and boots. We unload the snowmobile and she hops on the back. The trail isn't very busy, what with it being a weekday.

With her arms secure around my middle, I start the machine and we head into the woods. This is one of my favorite trails around this area. I'm pretty conservative at first since I'm not sure how comfortable Brinley is doing the same activity that killed her grandparents. Although I have no idea how her husband died, I want her to enjoy herself, not frighten her.

"You can go faster," she says.

I laugh, revving the engine and speeding up. We go through trees, and I rest my hand on her leg as we make a turn I worry might tip us, but we come out of it fine. I relish having her body so close to mine for an hour until we get to a spot with a view of a glacier. We take off our helmets, and I go sit behind her so she's in front of me.

"It's amazing how beautiful nature is, isn't it?" she says.

"Sad the way the glaciers are melting."

She nods and looks back at me. "Thanks for taking me. It's been way too long since I've done something like this. On my day off, I'm usually with some family member. They like to pass me around like a hot potato ever since Sawyer died."

"Well, I'm glad you came, but the day's not over yet. Do you want to drive?"

She gets an excited look on her face. "Um… yeah!"

We put on our helmets, she starts the machine like a pro, and we're off without any warning. So much for me taking my time to increase our speed. She's a demon right out of the gate, even venturing off to the side of the path where there's fresh snow.

I revel in her laughter through the wind. The way her body knows exactly how to move. She'd ride my motorcycle like a pro. I wish the weather was warmer so I could take her out on my bike. I place my hand on her hip, and she slows us down through an opening in the trees, pointing toward a moose in the middle.

We watch it since we're far enough away, and it doesn't see us yet. It's busy eating snow and just looking around.

She starts back up, going slowly, but quickly increases her speed once we're away from the moose. She drives for about an hour, then we're back at the truck.

She stands and takes off her helmet. "That was so fun. Thank you."

I remove my jacket because I'm sweating, then I get the snowmobile up on my trailer. She helps me secure it by taking one side and I take the other. We work as a team.

I try not to think too much about the warmth spreading throughout my chest at the thought that this is what life is about. Having someone to share these moments with. The glacier, the moose, the memory that will always make me think of Brinley. All these years I've been solo, telling stories to my buddies about what I've seen, not having anyone else to share the memory with.

We strip out of our snow pants and jackets and climb into the truck to get warm. She immediately puts her hands by the heater, but I take them in my own and blow on them, rubbing them to get them warmer quicker. Our eyes catch, and she has a soft, gentle smile. And then a grin that says a million different things but mostly how much she appreciates today.

"You were even more beautiful out there. There's a side of Brinley Kelly I didn't know existed."

She laughs. "Yeah, I'm kind of a thrill seeker like my dad. But I haven't done anything like that since Sawyer died."

I want to ask her how he died, but I don't want to upset her by asking her to relive such an awful time in her life. I'll be patient, and I'm sure she'll tell me when she's ready.

"You were in your element for sure. Hopefully, you'll

think the same of our next adventure." She tilts her head and I turn to the steering wheel to buckle in. "It's a surprise."

I drive us twenty minutes to a parking lot filled with firetrucks and ambulances parked along the fire lanes.

"What is this?" she asks, but as we grow closer, she sees the signs for the Polar Plunge. "Seriously?"

"You game?"

She bites her lip. "Yeah, but it's my first time."

"Me too. We'll do it together." I hold my hand out for her, and she puts her hand in mine. I squeeze it. "Let's go."

She nods and we exit the truck, walking up to sign our release forms.

The sign on the table reads, Annual Polar Plunge for the Special Olympics. I cannot believe I'm about to jump into a lake that was carved out, but here goes nothing.

Van hands me a package on the way to the sign-up.

"What's this?"

"What you'll have to wear."

I lift the yellow bikini out of the bag. "Are you insane? It's freezing."

"I'm only wearing board shorts," he says as though that's comparable.

"If you wear a speedo, then I'm game. Otherwise, I am not going in a bikini." I cross my arms.

He blows out a breath, looking around. "I don't have a choice. I didn't buy a speedo."

I eye his lower half because I saw his boxer briefs the other night, and he doesn't wear the super long ones. He must prefer the short version that's only, like, three inches down his leg and they are tight in the best way.

He shakes his head with a chuckle. "Deal."

"Really?" I do a little dance.

"Come on." He pulls on my hand and leads us to the table.

The people are super nice and Van hands them a check as our pledges for entry. I'm not sure how much it is, but the woman's eyes bulge out and she passes it to another woman and touches his arm while filling out the form, thanking him.

"Happy to help," he says with one of his easygoing smiles.

I sign my name, releasing them of all liability. We're told to go inside a giant tent where there are private stalls to change, then come out with our bag of clothes and towels or whatever and go to the edge of the lake for our turn. She explains there are firefighters in the water in diving gear in case something bad happens, but all we have to do is jump in and swim to the other side with the ladders and climb out. There's another tent on the other side where there are hot tubs to warm us up.

"But as we all know, body heat is the best way to warm up." The woman winks at us.

I'm sure my face is bright red and not from the cold.

Van picks up his duffel bag he left on the ground while filling out the papers and we go to the prep tent. Since we've seen each other naked—and thanks to the bikini he got me, I'll need his help tying it around my back—we change in the same stall.

"I cannot believe you bought this for me. Do men know that sometimes a one-piece can be just as sexy?" I take off my jeans, already feeling the crispness of the air on my skin. "Plus, what if I didn't shave?"

"Did you?" he asks, stripping off his sweatshirt and unbuckling his pants.

"Yes."

"Why?" He bites his lip and looks at me.

"Because we were going on a date and women shave before dates."

"I heard only if..."

I shake my head. Of course I shaved in case we slept together. After the other night on the couch and then the shower, we're so close, and he's been so great about waiting. But he doesn't need to know that. "I guess you'll have to find out, but next time you take a woman on a date to a Polar Plunge, some warning would be nice."

He chuckles but pulls down his jeans, and the small space between us heats despite the time of year. His boxer briefs are typical black ones, just like the other night, and his dick bulge is substantial—even in the cold.

"Stop staring at me because I'm not going out there with a hard-on." He folds his clothes and mine and puts them in the duffel bag before taking out two giant beach towels.

"I need you to tie me up," I say, pulling the two straps to my back and turning around.

"I'll tie you up anytime. All you have to say is please."

I shiver from the deep timbre of his voice, and he takes the straps and ties them around my back, then tightens the one around my neck.

"So how do I look?" I put my hands out at my sides.

"I think I should've gone with a wetsuit for you."

I playfully smack him, pick up my towel, and wrap it around my body as though I just got out of the shower. He ties his around his waist, showing off his chest. The minute we step out, the rest of the tent grows silent from all the women gawking at him.

We get in line, and he possessively puts his arm around

my waist, keeping me by his side, which I'm not going to complain about. I'm happy to let these women know we're together. Plus, he's kind of keeping me warm.

The line inches along, and the screams of the people jumping into the water make me feel as if I'm at a haunted house, and the screams are a warning of what I'm in for.

Before I'm ready—of course, I'm not sure I would ever be ready—we're at the front of the line. We talk to some guy who asks us our names and where we're from. I'm surprised when Van says Lake Starlight along with me, but I guess that's accurate right now.

"Stay warm, although I have a feeling you two don't have a problem with that. Oh, to be young again."

We laugh.

"It's your turn. Go jump." He puts out his arm in the direction we need to go.

Suddenly, my feet freeze in place, and not just from the snow I'm standing on.

Van doesn't accept me having last-minute doubts. "Just imagine how you'll feel when it's all over. That adrenaline high."

"Or death."

"Look at Ken and Barbie here," a fireman yells.

"Malibu Ken and Barbie, you mean," someone corrects him.

They all laugh.

"Just tell us when to jump," I grumble when I really want to ask how jealous they are of Van's body. But they're the ones who will save us if something happens, so I keep my mouth shut.

"Okay, brave ones, on three." The guy on the microphone counts down for us. "One... two... three."

We jump and I'm consumed by the cold water. All the

air rushes out of my lungs, and when I come to the surface, my body is numb. Once my voice is working, I scream. Shaking like a pile driver, I make it over to the ladder and the fireman high-fives me as I grab it and walk up. Once Van's out, he grabs my towel, wrapping it around me before he takes care of himself. We run to the tent with the hot tubs, and I drop my towel before jumping into the closest one.

"Oh my god, that feels so good. Too good." I squat as low as I can and Van steps into the hot tub as though it wasn't that bad. "Are you trying to act like some tough guy?"

He smirks, sitting down, so I swim over and cozy up on his lap. There aren't too many people in here right now, and I'm only sitting on his lap.

He wraps his arms around my waist and kisses my temple. "You okay?"

I look up and nod. "It was exhilarating. At first I couldn't breathe from how cold it was, but then I felt refreshed, and then I was freezing cold. But this... this is nice." I run my hands over his body that's slowly warming up.

"It is nice. I wish it was our own personal one." His hands slide around my stomach.

I become hyperaware that I'm barely wearing anything. The fabric that separates our bodies is minimal. Sexual hunger roars up inside me.

A large group comes in after us, so I slide off his lap to sit beside him, and he takes my hand. His thumb runs along the length of my thumb and it's as if he's strumming my libido because I'm anxious and needy for his touch in other places. I'm not even sure what's come over me, but I'm about to straddle him even with witnesses.

"Brin," he says, his first time using my nickname. He must notice the lust in my eyes because he tilts his head. Then he turns to the other people. "I think she's still warming up. We're from Lake Starlight."

My mind hiccups at the word *we're*. Both of us, as if *we're* a couple. I haven't been part of a *we're* in a long time, and I forgot how much I loved it. To be a *we*, not a *me*.

The woman carries on about how she loves to come to downtown Lake Starlight to all the little shops and restaurants and how much her kids love Founder's Day with the carnival and parade.

Van smiles and agrees, although he hasn't had to endure Founder's Day yet and probably won't since it happens in spring. My family puts it on for the town and I end up on a float, singing. It hasn't really been the same since Great-Grandma Dori died, but now there's a picture of her and great-grandpa Phillip on one float and my grandparents' picture on another. One day they'll have to start combining the floats because there are just too many of us Baileys.

"Ready?" I whisper, unable to stop my mind from swirling and really wanting to be alone with Van.

"Warm enough?"

I nod, although I could stay in here all day.

"You two make a great couple. Have a safe trip back to Lake Starlight," the woman says, waving.

We both smile and wave back, but I wrap my towel around myself, put on my boots, and tell Van I'll change in the truck.

We make a run for the truck, and Van starts it immediately, cranking the heat. I climb into his lap and straddle him, pressing my body against his. Thankfully, we had to park a little out from everyone else since the parking was full when we arrived.

"Whoa," he says.

"Didn't you hear what that lady said? This is how we're supposed to stay warm, body heat."

"Definitely, but we should take off our wet clothes first."

I kiss his neck, running my body up and down on his as if I'm a cat with an itch I can't scratch. "Then strip me, Van," I say softly, and he inhales deeply.

His fingers skim my skin around my back and untie both sets of strings. I draw back and allow the fabric to fall off my body. Van watches with avid interest once I'm bared to him.

"Put your hands on me. Warm them up."

"My pleasure." He does just that, his big hands molding to my tits and brushing my nipples.

I moan from the pleasure of his touch on my body. But I want more. I'm eager to feel all of him. "I want you."

"Here?" His eyes widen. "Brinley..."

I draw back from him and cradle his cheeks in my hands. I smile at how concerned he looks. I didn't think it would be like this either, but I don't need rose petals and champagne and a king-size bed. "I just want you. Please."

He stares at me for a long beat, and I expect him to refuse me, say it should be special or some crap, but he thumbs toward the back seat. "Get in the back," he says with authority.

Hot damn. I smash my lips against his, giving it everything I have to tell him he made the right choice. That it doesn't matter where, as long as it's him and me.

I strip my mouth off him because I'm eager for what's to come. I crawl in the back, lay down the towel, and take off my swim bottoms. He hurriedly gets out and joins me in the back, then takes off his boxer briefs and lays them on the floor before his body lies over mine.

I moan, my hands running up and down his back. "You feel so good."

He pushes the hair off my forehead. "Are you sure?"

"Positive."

He nods as if he's convincing himself, then he lowers his weight onto me and places his lips on mine. It's the starting gun because slow and sure is not going to be the pace of this race. This one will be a sprint to the finish.

twenty-four

BRINLEY

His body is all hard planes and strength, but his hands are pure magic.

"I don't have anything with me," he whispers. "I'm not prepared." Disappointment weeps from his eyes, but I have a feeling it's more because he's letting me down than for his benefit.

"When was the last time you were with someone?"

"God, a while ago and I've always used a condom, but—"

"We're good. I'm still on the pill. I mean, as long as you're okay with it?" The question floats in the air. I don't want to stop. I want to feel him, all of him.

"As long as you are, I am."

I nod rapidly. "I am."

He bends down, hovering his lips over mine. "Before we do this, I want to put a disclaimer out there. No matter where we're at, you say stop, and I stop. Don't ever put my feelings into consideration, understand?"

I nod, my hands running over his short, damp hair. Instead of kissing me, his lips fall to my neck.

"You have no idea how long I've wanted to sink inside of you, and now I'm a bit nervous." He nibbles my skin down the front of my neck, and I bend back from him as much as I can.

How can this strong-as-steel man voice his vulnerability to me? It makes me like him even more.

"I feel like I'm five years old, and I've stood in a long line outside the candy store. Now that I'm inside, I want it all. If I go too fast, just tell me."

"Stop with the disclaimers and fuck me, Van."

His tip breaches my opening, teasing my entrance. "My fucking pleasure."

His hands cradle my face, and his lips move to mine, his tongue gliding along the seam of my mouth. Heat buzzes under my skin and the kiss is like a steam engine, slow at first, but soon our mouths are colliding, our teeth gnashing as our hands seek out any piece of flesh to latch on to. His hands end up under my ass, and one of my legs stretches across the front seat, the other lifted on the headrest as he drags the tip of him through my wetness.

"You couldn't be any wetter," he says, watching himself.

"Please fuck me, Van."

He pushes into me, then seconds later, a full plunge before drawing it out again.

"Oh god," I moan.

The feeling is agonizingly addicting, and when he runs the pad of his thumb in circles over my clit, my ass bolts off the seat cushion, and I grip the towel under me, fisting it.

His thumb runs back and forth as he rocks inside me. Every nerve in my body is screaming for relief, but I'm not ready for this to be over. I don't want a flood of emotions to hit me when this ends. I just want to enjoy Van and being with him. As selfish as it is, I don't want Sawyer leaking into this moment.

"Play with your tits," Van says. "I want to watch you."

As always, he knows when I'm becoming lost in my head, so he gave me a task. I place my hands on my tits, playing with my nipples, pinching, pulling, and staring at him while he watches me. When his vision shifts from my hands to where he's driving into me, I run my hands down his muscular chest and around to his ass. It clenches in my grip, the firmness of it not surprising me.

He falls forward, and I hold him down on top of me as he drills inside me. "God, you're so perfect," he whispers, kissing my neck and my shoulder. "I never want this to be over. I want to live inside of you forever."

My eyes fall shut because I feel the exact same way. I couldn't be happier that we didn't wait until the day he was going to leave because to think this would be our only time feels crushing. I need more of him. I want to taste him, feel him come down my throat. I want to feel that stubble between my thighs and try every position imaginable. Hell, make up new ones.

"I'm so close. Harder." My fingertips push into his ass cheeks.

Instead of picking up the pace like I thought he might, he slows his rhythm with long drags out and quick thrusts in, hitting me in exactly the right way. And just like that, my orgasm isn't just on the cusp of coming. It's building layer by layer with every drag of his cock sheathed in my wetness. His mouth explores every inch of my skin, murmuring praise over my body. His breathing is staggered, almost broken as if he's right where I am.

I run my fingernails up and down his back and across his shoulder blades. I tighten my walls, pushing back my orgasm, and he growls in my ear, sucking on my earlobe as he slams into me. Suddenly, he's not taking the long drags out of me, but quick thrusts and his arms wrap around my body, using the force to drive his dick down. He's so far inside me, I scream from pleasure.

"Take the fall, Brin. I promise I'll catch you."

His whispered words make me come apart, my body tensing as my orgasm hits me with brute force and catapults me over an imaginary cliff so that I'm free-falling. Before I fall into the abyss, his lips smash to mine, and he jolts inside me and stills as he comes, leaking out onto my thighs.

We lie there, our breathing ragged and trying to find its rhythm again. He rises up and brushes the wet strands from my forehead. He doesn't ask me anything, but I know he's checking to make sure I'm okay. There are no tears and no regrets. I kiss him and he smiles.

"You're a temptress." He rises off me, and when he slips out of me, he uses the towel to clean me up, then himself.

"Who knew plunging into cold water was an aphrodisiac?" I laugh.

He digs into the duffel bag, handing me my clothes. "I hate that we have to get dressed and go."

"We can go home, order some takeout, and do it all over again," I say, and he turns his head and looks at me. "What?"

He captures my bottom lip with his teeth, pulling me closer before he kisses me thoroughly. "Nothing. Sounds perfect."

We both get dressed and climb into the front seat. Well, I climb. He gets out and back in. We wait a few minutes for the steam to disappear from the windows, then we make the trip back to Lake Starlight, hand in hand.

My stomach flips every time I think about being with him. And although Sawyer did slip into my mind momentarily, I wasn't overcome with grief or guilt. I have no idea how to describe the feeling inside me, but it's almost freeing, as if I dropped a backpack full of bricks I've been carrying for years.

***

WE GOT HOME and took a shower, then dressed in our pajamas—me with no underwear and him in pajama pants with no shirt and no underwear. We got Wok For U and ate out of the cartons, watching a little of *The Mindy Project*, but our hands were too busy roaming each other's bodies to pay attention to what was going on.

Now I have my sketchbook and I'm sitting across the room on the chair while Van lies on the couch naked, trying to look as though he's not trying to be sexy. He's failing miserably.

"You said you'd model, so sit still." I use my pencil to fix one of my lines.

"No one will ever see this, correct?" This is the tenth time he's asked.

"It's a very complimentary drawing."

"I do not want a naked picture of me out there."

"It's a drawing. Now relax. I have to get your abs right."

He finally quiets down and lies still for me. The only sound for a while is my pencil on the sketchpad, and it's calming to me.

"Have you drawn anything since I got it for you?" he asks.

I nod, my eyes not leaving the paper. "I have."

"What?"

I shrug. "Some flowers, some shapes, objects. No faces or anything."

"Does sketching make you happy?"

"Yes." I smile and look up at him.

He shoots me a smile back. "Ever thought of tattooing like your dad?"

I shake my head, eyes wide. "No way. The idea of being the one to put something permanent on someone's skin is terrifying. They mean a lot to some people. I mean, my mom and her siblings all have this one tattoo that my dad drew to honor their parents. My dad said it was when he first knew he had a chance with my mom—when she came to him for a tattoo that meant so much to her. Although they still didn't get together for years. But I mean, like, your tattoos, how did you trust the person?"

He glances at his arms. "Usually you've seen their work or you hear about them from a friend. Your dad has a great reputation. A few of my friends have come here just to get him to work on them."

"Really?" I guess I never thought of my dad as having a fan base. I mean, everyone in Lake Starlight loves him because he's Liam Kelly and does anything for anyone. "That's kind of cool."

"I think so. Maybe I'll get him to do something for me before I leave."

I cough and cover my mouth. "Maybe wait on that just a bit."

It's not that my dad doesn't like Van, he doesn't really know him, but he worries that Van isn't the type of person for me. Mostly because he thinks I should be with someone like Sawyer.

Dad thought Sawyer was great. Reliable, steady, and stable were his words for him. That was after they got over the fact I was marrying so young. Dad looked at me before he walked me down the aisle, while I was a ball of nerves thinking everyone was right and maybe we were making a mistake. My dad said, "I'll never have to worry about you. He's a good one. I couldn't have picked better myself."

"I should talk to him," Van says. "It's not right that I'm sleeping with his daughter, and he barely knows me."

"It's not like we're dating. You're leaving soon, and after that, it won't matter."

We're both quiet for a beat as the reality of that sets in.

"I'll just be the douchebag who hurt his daughter."

"Hey," I say. "Look at me." His gaze meets mine. "I'm fine. I will be fine. Stop worrying that you're such a great catch I'll crumble into pieces the minute you leave." I roll my eyes playfully. More playful than I actually feel.

He swallows hard. "Are you almost done?"

"Almost." I continue to sketch his hair and his full lips and sharp jaw. I go over his dick again and make sure his thighs reflect the muscle and strength there. "Done."

"Do I get to see it?"

"No. That wasn't part of the deal."

I go to my room and am about to shove the sketchbook in a drawer when his heavy footsteps fall behind me. Van wraps his arm around my waist and then tosses me on the bed, tickling me until I finally drop the sketchbook. I try to grab the book, but he gets a hold of my hands and holds them above my head as he flips the pages with one hand, the sketchbook resting on the bed.

He picks up the book and inspects the drawing I just did. "I think I'm bigger than that," he says dryly.

"I gave you a nine-inch dick."

He flips through the pages I worked on before today's

session and gets to the only one I did by memory—our two hands entwined together.

"You have a gift," he says. "You need to be doing this."

I shake my head, take the sketchbook, and drop it on the floor. He hovers over me, holding my hands over my head still, then he slides down my body, his tongue trailing a path until he nestles between my legs.

"If I make you come, you turn in your notice to your mom," he says, his wry smile telling me he's joking.

"I wish. It'll take a lot more than a few sketches for that to happen."

He shrugs. "Okay, I'll still make you come."

I laugh, but he licks along my slit and sucks my clit into his mouth. Damn, is there anything this man doesn't do to perfection?

twenty-five

VAN

I t's my birthday, and I'm in a decent mood as I walk to work to start my shift. Brinley said she'd come by after she made a quick trip to Winterberry Falls for some chocolate cake. After my shift is done, she's going to spread it all over her body for me to lick off as a birthday gift.

Who could ask for anything better?

This past week, we've literally fucked everywhere in our apartment. Last night I was cooking dinner but stopped because she started kissing my neck and I had to have her. We can't get through one episode of *The Mindy Project* without stripping off our clothes, so we just gave up midweek. When I got home late one night, she'd left me a trail of her clothes to her bedroom, where I found her completely naked and her wrists cuffed to the bed frame. I'll never get that visual out of my head.

I'm in my head with that particular vision when I open the door to Lucky's, so it takes me a second to make sense of the "Happy Birthday" banner hanging across the bar.

A large group of people jump out and yell, "Surprise!"

The person front and center is my sneaky roommate and lover, Brinley. She walks right up to me and places her lips on mine. "Don't be upset, I really wanted to do this for you, and there's a chocolate cake ready for later."

"There better be. I'm going to spread it all over my dick for you," I murmur into her ear.

She laughs. "Deal."

Brinley takes my hand, and we make our way around the room, thanking everyone for the birthday wishes. I find out she paid to have the entire bar just for my party, inviting mostly her family, the Girl Scouts leader, and Alice and her gang. I recognize Jack from the hardware store and his wife. And a few more people I've met during my time here. Although I didn't want any of this, it's nice that she thought of me and that all of these people came to help me celebrate. God knows my own mother doesn't care that she birthed me today.

I'm talking to Brinley's uncle Kingston about the Polar Plunge we did last week, and he tells me that it's his fire department that handles that. He said they leave it to the rookies to stay in the water and that he might make an appearance now and then, but he's sorry he missed me.

"Did I hear that right? You two did the Polar Plunge?" Brinley's dad comes over and shakes Kingston's hand.

"Hey, Dad, you remember Van?" Brinley motions to me.

I hold out my hand. "Nice to see you again, sir."

"Call me Liam." He blows out a breath as though it kills him to say that. "How the hell did you convince Brinley to take the plunge?"

"I didn't. I took her snowmobiling, then to the Polar Plunge. She was excited to do it. No convincing involved."

Liam's eyes bulge out. "I'm shocked. I thought maybe that little daredevil side of you died a long time ago."

"You and Mom should do it, Dad. It's thrilling. Bitter cold, but they have hot tubs to jump in after to warm you—"

He raises his hands. "I'm over here being cordial because your mother put on a chastity belt until I make nice with Van. Save me the hot tub talk. I need to have a word with him, so go somewhere." He waves for Brinley to leave.

My balls scrunch up inside as I say a little prayer he doesn't injure them.

"Be nice, Dad," she says through gritted teeth.

"I'm the dad, I'm not supposed to be nice." Liam motions with his head to a vacant booth in the corner and I follow. I sip my beer and he does the same. "You're really becoming BuzzWheel famous around here. Back in my day, people didn't want to be on there, but they keep bragging about you. You'd think you know the writer or something."

I shake my head. "No, sir."

He gives me a look.

"No, Liam, I don't know anyone who writes for that app. I didn't even know it existed until Brinley told me."

"Do you always room with women?"

Man, he's a straight shooter.

"No." I laugh. "I'm usually with a large group of guys."

His forehead scrunches. "What does that mean? Are you bisexual?" Maybe I should've phrased it differently.

"I'm in the military."

He blinks, clearly surprised. "Oh, you're a veteran?"

I nod.

"Thank you for your service."

"Welcome." I'm not sure how specific I should get with him. Brinley and I never discussed if anyone else should know I'm leaving in a few weeks to go back to Kodiak, so I keep my mouth shut about it.

"Last time we talked, you said you weren't going to try to get in my daughter's pants, but here she is throwing you a birthday party and kissing you when you come in. She's sitting in your lap by the bonfire, and you take her to do a Polar Plunge. I'm not an idiot, I know the two of you are sleeping together."

I don't say anything right away because he's right. I told him I wouldn't, and I did. I've already betrayed his trust. "I'm sorry, it just happened. But honestly, if I could turn back time, I'd do it all over again. She's amazing. And I know I'm undeserving of her, but… she's impossible to resist."

His eyebrows rise, and he finishes his drink, staring at me and not saying anything. The longer he doesn't say anything, the more I worry. Then he puts his hand out between us, and I shake it before he changes his mind.

"You sound way too much like myself when I was younger to give you any more grief. But… you know she's a widow?"

I nod.

"I do see the changes in her. You're pulling out the girl she was before she learned life can be brutally unfair. Her mother and I would like to thank you for that."

Damn, this conversation took a different turn than I thought it would. "It's not me. Only she has control of that."

"But she's trusting you enough to be vulnerable and show you the real her and that's what matters. Her mom had her guard up when I decided to try my fate with her. They can be hard nuts to crack."

"Did you just call me a nut?" Savannah comes by and puts her arm around her husband.

He kisses her. "We're good here, so you can give me the key to that chastity belt now."

I want to put my fingers in my ears, but I smack on a fake smile.

"Oh good, you're done." Brinley puts her arm through mine. "Let me rescue you before they start making out."

"Thanks for the talk, Liam. Nice to see you, Savannah." I nod.

"You're welcome. We won't be here long, so happy birthday," Liam says, and I'm pretty sure I catch him grabbing a handful of his wife's ass before I turn back around.

Brinley drags me to the pool table, where we find most of her cousins. For the rest of the night, we play pool. Brinley and I hustle Easton and Lance. Calista and Rylan leave early while a few of her other cousins linger. They all wish me a happy birthday, and when Brinley brings out the cake, I can't believe how many people are singing.

I can't help but think that this is what the commander was talking about. But that thought is followed by the realization that these are the same people who would worry about me every time the helicopter gets called. Why would I put anyone I care about through that? Still, it's nice to feel so liked. And I can tell how happy Brinley's family is watching her with me as if her wounds are all healed.

BRINLEY and I walk home after Nate and Sabrina say they'll clean up. She's holding a small bag.

"What's that?" I ask.

"My decorations." She gives me a coy smile.

I take her hand, tugging her toward our building. We run up the stairs and unlock the apartment door before we shut it and lock ourselves inside. My lips land on hers, and I press her back against the door. She meets me with the same fervor, grabbing the hem of my shirt and tugging it up my torso. I grab it by the collar and rip it off my body.

"Wait," she murmurs along my lips. "I have to get ready for you."

She takes the bag and goes into her room. I pace for what seems like forever.

Finally her soft voice says, "Ready."

I open the door and find her on the bed with streaks of chocolate frosting along her body. She's trailed it down her stomach, across her tits, dollops on her nipples, and I can't wait to see where else.

I strip off my jeans and socks and put one knee on the bed. "I'll never look at chocolate cake the same way again."

I take one of her legs and rest it on my shoulder, slowly licking the trail of frosting leading up her leg until I'm eye level with her pussy. I press a kiss to her mound and she moans, then I bring her other leg up in the air and lick the frosting down to her ankle.

After I'm done, I hover over her. "Where should I lick next?"

Her teeth press into her bottom lip as I dip my head and extend my tongue, flicking the frosting from her collarbone into my mouth. My finger traces the frosting on her nipple, and I take it and smear it on her lips.

"You missed my favorite spot." I kiss her, the two of us making a mess with frosting all over our lips.

I continue down her body, savoring her tits, worshiping her nipples. I don't want to go fast tonight. I want us to slow it down, savor this because my days here are numbered, and soon, all I'll have are memories of these intimate moments.

"Want me to put some on your dick for me to lick off?" she asks.

"Later." I run a hand along her hairline and stare at her beautiful face. I'm so worried the memory of her will fade after I leave. I kiss her, sliding my tongue into her mouth, then roll us so that she's straddling me because I want to stare at her while I'm inside her. "Slide me in, baby."

She rises up, grabs the base of my dick and sinks down on it.

"That's it, baby. Rock on it."

She moves her hips, her hands on my chest and our eyes locked as the pleasure builds. I fondle her tits, running my fingers over her nipples. They harden further from my touch. I commit every part of her to memory. She rises and then slides back down. I raise my hips, meeting her halfway so I can be as deep inside her as possible.

"God, Van, you always feel so good."

"You too. Like fucking silk."

She works me at a slow pace, tension thick in the air because we're not just fucking. We both know we're not crazed, only looking for our orgasms. We're drawing it out because we don't want this feeling of connection to vanish.

Because when I leave here, I'm going to feel hollow and empty. She's filled my life with so much happiness.

"Brin?" I ask, rocking my hips up. Her eyes flutter open. "Maybe we can... I mean, I'm not *that* far away. Maybe we can work something out."

Her face doesn't show she even heard me at first, then a smile shines down on me like sunshine. She falls to my chest, her lips on mine, her hands on my cheeks. "I was thinking the same thing."

I roll us over and slide in and out of her, my eyes never leaving hers. I've never been so happy. I have no idea of the logistics, but I can't say goodbye to her. Can't bear not knowing what's going on in her life. We have to figure this out because she's ruined me.

"I'm almost there," she says, panting.

"Me too." I increase the tempo, and she comes on a cry that I swallow with a kiss as I pour into her.

My head is in the crook of her neck when a wet drop lands on my temple. I quickly pick up my head to see tears falling down her cheeks. Shit. I thought we were in the clear.

twenty-six

VAN

"Fuck, Brin, what's wrong?" I ask, climbing up on the bed to rest my back on the headboard and holding her in my arms.

She shakes her head. "I never thought I could be this happy again."

"You scared the shit out of me. I thought you were regretting this or what we said about figuring out how to be together."

She shakes her head and wipes her tears. "I thought I was tough enough to say goodbye to you, but I'm not. When I was planning your birthday party, my cousins were all over me about how happy I seemed, and it really made me think. Then I thought about you leaving, and well, I couldn't even fathom going on with my life as if you were never part of it. Sure, there're memories, but those fade. I should know, I barely remember the day of Sawyer's death." She pulls back a bit and looks at me. "That's something we haven't talked about."

I tighten my arms around her shoulders. "You don't have to."

"I really want to, but I don't want to ruin your birthday."

I smile. "Nothing can ruin tonight for me. I'm honored you trust me enough to share."

She turns around and sits up on her knees to face me, her fingers fiddling with one another. I grab her hands and run my thumbs over them.

"He worked in investments and went out with a lot of clients who always had a lot of toys—personal planes, fancy penthouses in New York. But he also had clients from Alaska who had gotten rich on oil and didn't do the luxury lifestyle, but still had expensive things like big fishing boats and four runners and snowmobiles, cabins in remote areas."

"Sounds nice," I say.

"Sometimes I got invited, but mostly it was guys' trips, especially with his clients from Alaska. They'd hunt, fish, camp, go on excursions with tour companies. He needed to keep them happy, especially when their investments were trending the wrong way. Anyway, we'd been married just over a year when he told me he had to go on a big fishing trip with one of his clients."

My stomach clenches because I know all too well how many "fishermen" we've saved from their own stupidity of not knowing the weather they're going out in. You'd think as rich as they are, they'd hire actual fishermen, but their egos are always too big.

"It was like any other time. He was going to be gone for a few days and he said when he returned, he'd carve some time out for us to go away for our one-year anniversary."

She stops speaking, and I continue to rub her hands.

"It was early one morning when there was a knock on

my door. I figured it was one of my family members, but it was Sheriff Miller Jr. and another officer. They informed me there had been an accident and Sawyer had died. They asked if I could go with them to identify Sawyer's body. I called my parents, who, of course, came with me. His body had been flown to Anchorage and was in the morgue there. It was all so surreal. I was in the back of my dad's car, and my mom just kept asking me questions I didn't have answers to. I never asked where they went or any specifics. He'd always just gone and returned."

A few tears run down her cheeks, and I wipe them away. I bet one of my buddies was dispatched, or maybe it all happened too late for us to reach them and it was only a recovery, not a rescue. "Brin…"

She shakes her head. "I'm sorry. I was just this naive little wife who never asked questions and assumed he'd show up like he was supposed to."

"You expected him to come home. And nine point nine times out of ten, that's what happens. You can't beat your-self up about that."

She grants me a small tilt of her head. "I don't even know what happened. The accident, how they got him, or if they ever saw him alive. No one really told me anything, and at the time, I didn't ask because I was in such a state of shock."

An eerie feeling creeps over me, like a sudden knowing deep in my gut as my heart hammers.

"What do you remember?" I ask, my voice shaking.

"They just said there was a fire on the boat and the boaters tried to get it out themselves, probably waited too long before calling in the Mayday. They were far out, and it took over an hour for the Coast Guard to get there. The boat was still on fire and hadn't sunk yet. When the Coast Guard showed up, they were on the deck, waving their hands. A diver was sent down, and chaos erupted. The diver had to act based on who he could save, but in the end, he didn't save anyone. There were no survivors."

"Did you get an autopsy done?" I ask gently.

She nods. "Yeah. Cause of death was drowning, which I always thought was so weird because they had his body. If he drowned, shouldn't he be at the bottom of the ocean?"

I bite my lip because I know exactly how that happens. "Anything in his system?"

She nods. "Alcohol."

"Just alcohol?"

She shakes her head. "Cocaine. I never even knew he did that. But I kept that to myself. No one else knows."

I pull her into me and wrap my arms around her. I close my eyes, hoping she gives me a different answer than I'm expecting to the question I'm about to ask. "How long ago did this happen?"

"Four years ago," she says, and it feels as though someone threw an axe dead center in my chest.

I should've known life wouldn't give me Brinley—I don't deserve her.

BRINLEY FALLS asleep in my arms, and I lie in bed knowing I'm a selfish bastard for taking this night for myself. To hear her soft breaths and feel her arms clinging to me one last time.

I can't believe she's one of the widows. That incident was my first loss in the four years since I enrolled, and I've never gotten over it. I almost didn't reenlist after, but I went to therapy where they tell you to look at how many saves you've had, not how many losses. So when I reenlisted, I made a promise to myself that I would do anything in my power to make sure I didn't experience a loss like that again. And I did just that, dedicating myself to the job until it was my sole focus—which is how I ended up with my commander forcing me on eight weeks of leave.

It's easy for some therapist to tell you not to focus on the people you lose, but they don't know what it's like to be out there alone. How scared the people you're trying to help are, knowing you're in the middle of a dark ocean where Mother Nature makes the rules. The waves are high and deep and cold. Seeing the fear in a person's eyes makes you second-guess for one second why you'd choose this profession until you're both safe on the helicopter or boat after you've saved them. Their thank-yous and gratitude, seeing them reunited with their family, it all makes it worth it.

Sawyer should be in this bed with Brinley right now, not me, and it's my fault he's not. I'm a monster for holding her after what I did. She'll never forgive me once she knows, and why should she?

So I slide out from under her and pull the blanket up over her shoulders, then take one last look at her sleeping form before I slowly shut her bedroom door behind me. I throw on some clothes, pack my shit, and grab my keys.

I drive around for hours and come to the same conclusion as when I left—I need to tell her the truth.

I text her to tell her I have to go work out and I'll be back shortly. Since it's Saturday, she doesn't have to go to work. Then I call Calista, Easton, and Lance and ask them to meet me by the lake. They all complain, but they do as I ask. Thank God they gave me their numbers at my birthday party last night.

Lance is the first to show up. "Shit, man, I'm hungover. What do you need?"

"Just wait until everyone gets here."

We wait in silence, then he talks about how he's going to New York next week and how he should really get a condo there, but he likes his life here and wants to be like his dad. Then he goes into how maybe he should just buy a hotel around here and forget the family business, but his grandfather... I'm not really listening by that point.

Finally, Easton shows up with Calista right behind him, Rylan up on the hill. He's never too far from his wife. I'm sure I'd be the same way.

They all sit on benches their family donated, their family members' names on them. It must be nice to always be reminded of where you come from. I thought maybe I'd found that here, or at least with Brinley, but fate took a sharp turn.

"Out with it," Easton says.

"I don't want to get into specifics, but I'm about to go into my apartment and talk to Brinley. It's not going to go well, and after, I plan on leaving town."

"What the hell?" Calista says.

Easton and Lance stand to approach me.

I hold up my hands. "Brinley told me about how Sawyer died last night."

They're all still confused.

"Brinley doesn't know yet, but I'm a Coast Guard diver." I raise my eyebrows with the hopes they get it without me having to go into a big explanation. She deserves to find out first.

"Oh," Calista says. "Oh, and..."

I nod.

"Fucking hell," Easton says.

"Damn it," Lance echoes.

"I just need you guys to be there for her. I'm really sorry. If I'd known, I never would've started anything. I swear to you I didn't know."

They all nod, but they look as stunned as I was last night.

"Give me a half hour. You'll see me get in my truck." I push my hands into my jeans pockets and look at the ground.

"Are you sure you want to leave? I can arrange a room for you at the resort. Give both of you time to figure it out," Lance says.

I give him a sad smile. "I appreciate the offer, but..." I shake my head, not sure how to explain it. "I've felt guilty ever since the accident. I've wondered about the people left behind—how it affected them, whether they were able to move on with their lives. And now I know. I've been living with the byproduct of my failure. How could she ever look at me the same again? How could I ever look at her the same way?"

"I'm sorry, this sucks." Easton is the one who says it, which surprises me.

"I think you should wait," Calista chimes in. "You guys can figure it out."

I smile politely. "I'm the reason she's a widow. My job is to save people in the water, and I failed that night. Regardless of specifics, I failed, and she'll always look at me and know that."

Without another word, I walk up the hill, shake hands with Rylan—although he knows nothing of what is going on—and go back to my truck. I drive the few blocks to our apartment and park outside, not wasting any more time.

When I walk back into the apartment, Brinley looks up at me from the couch. "Hey you, I missed you this morning." Then she must register the anguish on my face and my bloodshot eyes. "What's wrong?"

"We need to talk."

twenty-seven

VAN

She walks over to me and wraps her arms around my waist, but I don't reciprocate the hug, guiding her back to the couch while I sit in the chair.

"Do you have a picture of Sawyer?" I ask, wanting to be sure. It's a last-ditch effort that won't pan out for me.

With a furrowed brow, she goes to a drawer, then hands me their wedding photo. Of course, those dark eyes staring at me in the photo are the lifeless ones that looked up at me on the helicopter.

"Why do you want this?" she asks softly.

I set the picture on the coffee table, looking up at her through my eyelashes and waiting for her to react. "Brinley, I'm a Coast Guard diver."

"And?" She sounds hopeful, like maybe I knew the diver or had heard about Sawyer's accident.

"I was the diver on scene the night Sawyer died. I was the one there."

"Oh." She looks away from me, looking lost.

"I'm the reason he's dead." The words feel like rocks in my mouth.

Her head slowly turns back to me, and her eyes narrow. "What? He drowned."

I lean forward and take her hands because this is probably the last time I will ever hold them. "Do you want me to tell you what happened that night? It's up to you, but either way, I've packed my stuff up and…" I dig into my pocket and pull out the check that covers the rest of the year. The good thing about having no life and not taking time off for years is that it really helps your savings account. "Here's the rest of the rent for the year."

"You're leaving?" Her eyes brim with tears.

"Did you hear me? It was me. The reason Sawyer is dead is me. I'm to blame."

"Did you know that when you came here?" she whispers.

I shake my head. "I didn't know until last night when you told me the story."

She nods and looks at her hands.

"Do you want me to tell you what happened that night?" Part of me wants to race out of here, and the other wants to take every last second I have remaining with her.

"Yes, tell me. I want to know."

I give a sharp nod. "Okay."

Our eyes lock, and she lifts her chin a bit as if putting on a brave face.

I figure she's ready, so I begin. "We were dispatched late, and as you already know, it took us over an hour to reach them. The weather wasn't horrible, the seas weren't crazy like they are in the winter, but it's still the ocean. When I arrived, three of them were on the deck. The helicopter lowered, and I jumped into the ocean. Thankfully, although they were all drunk, one got the ladder for me to climb onto the boat. But once I got there, it was pure chaos.

One man had a gash on his head and a significant burn on his arm, and another was running around, still trying to put out the fire. I made all three of them put a life preserver on and radioed to the chopper to lower the basket so I could put the man with the injuries on it. It wasn't Sawyer.

"When the basket lowered while I was tending to the injured man, trying to get the bleeding under control, Sawyer and the other guy fought over the basket. I had to leave the guy with the wound and go over to them. The one man was offering me crazy amounts of money to put him up first, but the injured go first. I explained it would be his friend but that there was no rush, we'd get everyone off."

I hate retelling this night in general, but there's an extra level of anxiety knowing we're about to come to the worst part and I'm talking to Sawyer's widow.

"Still with me?"

She nods though she's barely blinking, looking a little shell-shocked.

"So, I grabbed the basket again and was getting the injured guy into the basket when the guy offering me money jumped and clung onto the basket along with the injured guy. The injured man fell in the water. I dove in to get the guy, but the other guy couldn't hang on to the basket and fell in the water too. Meaning I now had two in the water and Sawyer still on the boat. We had another helicopter on the way, but they were thirty minutes out. We'd been dispatched because we were out on a training exercise, and we were the closest."

I pause and take a deep breath, hating this next part.

"Even if it's not winter, the water is freezing, and their clothes were no match for the ocean. I finally managed to get the one guy back on the boat and then go back for the injured guy, radioing for the chopper to lower the basket again. I figured I was safe to hook him in the water, but just as it got to me, Sawyer and the other guy jumped in, swimming toward us to get to the basket first. I've witnessed people get panicky before. They don't want to be left alone, and human nature takes over and it's every man for himself. The other guy pulled off his life preserver—I think in an effort to make it easier to swim so he'd beat Sawyer there. I'm sure the alcohol and drugs didn't help with the decision-making. But if we had done it orderly, it would have all been fine."

"Keep going," she says, showing signs of life again.

"I didn't get the injured man in the basket because Sawyer and the other guy got in. But both of their weights were too heavy, and the basket snapped off, and they hit the water hard. Sawyer came back up because he still had his life preserver on, but the other guy didn't. I dove under a few times but couldn't find him. Then I got a call on the radio that the chopper was low on fuel. I swam toward the boat with Sawyer in one hand and the injured guy in the other. It seemed like it took forever, and then the boat made a noise I could hear over the whirling of the helicopter blades, and I knew it was gonna go down. I don't know how to explain it, but when you've done the job for a while, sometimes you just know."

I take another breath, but she seems anxious for me to go on, so I do.

"I asked Sawyer if he could swim on his own and all three of us swam out. The helicopter lowered another basket down and I put the injured guy in. He was older and definitely not as strong as Sawyer. Sawyer could tread water and I would help him until they got his friend up. But Sawyer grabbed the clip, trying to get it on. I had no choice but to fight him for it, but then I lost the injured guy when a big wave came in and he floated away from me. By the time I'd gotten him and come back, Sawyer was ripping off his life jacket and his shirt."

When Brinley looks at me as though she doesn't understand, I explain. "Sometimes when people have hypothermia, they feel hot because their blood vessels are dilating to try to warm freezing tissue in their limbs. Very often people will strip out of their clothes in an effort to cool down and end up speeding up the process." I frown, hating that I'm having to give her that visual. "At this point, the boat was about to go down and you never really know which way they'll sink. So I grabbed the clip, strapped in the injured man, and they hoisted him up. A lot of good that did—he died of exposure on route back to land. Once he was headed up, I went to grab Sawyer to get him when the basket came back down, but he wasn't anywhere to be found. I dove under and saw him sinking. Brinley?"

"I'm fine, just continue. I want to know." Her voice is hoarse.

"I grabbed his arm and pulled him up, but when we surfaced, a big wave came and it took a minute to get my bearings. The pilot said we were low on fuel and had to go now. When I got him up, his body was limp, and I had an idea we'd lost him. The guys tried CPR once he was in the chopper, but it was no use. He was gone. Too much time in the water, too much water in his lungs. As we were flying away, the ship was barely above the water."

She looks at me, and I inhale a deep breath.

"I went from never losing anyone to losing three. We never recovered the third body. What I don't understand, though, is that there was no Sawyer lost that day. I've read the incident reports enough times to know."

She nods slowly, almost as if she's in a trance. "His

given name was Bartholomew. It's a terrible name. He never used it. Went by his middle name instead." She lets out a sad sort of laugh. "Kind of like you."

I wince. "I'm so sorry it was Sawyer, Brinley. I hope someday you can forgive me." I stand. "I've already packed my things, and they're in the truck."

She stares at her hands. "Thank you." She stands. "For telling me. I've always wondered what happened that night. If he was in pain and how he drowned when they recovered his body."

I run my hand down her cheek. "I wish it was different. My time with you has been the best in my life. Always know that. But had I known who you were, I never would've come here. I would never put you through this."

"I don't know what to say," she whispers.

"You don't need to say anything. I know this is too much for us to get over. You'll always see him when you look at me now, and I'll always see my failure to save three men when I look at you." I give her a questioning look and she doesn't tell me I'm wrong. I lean in and kiss her forehead. "Bye, Brinley."

I walk out of her apartment and down the stairs to my truck. Her cousins are waiting, and I toss Calista my keys to the apartment before I get in my truck.

I wait for them to walk into the building, an ache building in my chest because I'll never walk in there again. With my motorcycle and snowmobile attached to my trailer, I drive out of Lake Starlight, knowing it's carved a spot out of my heart. This town tattooed itself on me and I'll never forget it, but most of all, I'll never forget her.

twenty-eight

BRINLEY

I look over the BuzzWheel article again. There's a picture of Van's truck, his motorcycle and snowmobile attached to a trailer, driving over the city limits. The "Thanks for visiting Lake Starlight" sign is captured so perfectly you would've thought it was a staged shot.

WE THOUGHT *Van Adler would become a longtime resident of Lake Starlight, but he's left town with few answers this morning. After Brinley threw him a big birthday party last night, the two of them seemed as happy as any couple can, so we were shocked to hear that he's left town.*

The only news I have right now is that he met up with Easton Bailey, Lance Whitmore, and Calista Greene by the lake, then drove to his apartment and was inside for no more than a half hour. When he came out, Brinley's cousins went in and haven't left since.

I'm not sure we'll ever get more on the whys, but I think everyone's heart in Lake Starlight is breaking for our Brinley Kelly. She's had to endure too much heartbreak at too young of an age. She really looked happy last night. That's what my article was going to be about today, with some pictures of them as a couple, so this is a sad turn of events. We're with you, Brinley, here to see you through another heartbreak.

THE COMMENTS all say how they never really liked Van anyway, which is bullshit. Others say they always knew there was a sneaky side to him. And then there's a whole slew of them offering me condolences as if he died.

I toss the phone on the couch.

"I don't know why you're reading it again." Calista picks up the phone and closes the app.

"I really hate being Lake Starlight's charity case."

"Everyone is at one point or the other," Lance says. "My mom told me what it was like when she was the jilted bride."

"I just can't believe..." I can't even talk about it. "And then he just leaves me."

"I think he thought that's what you would want," Calista says. "That it would be too hard to look at him after you knew."

"You were still mourning Sawyer pretty bad when he came into your life." Easton changes the channel to another college football game. "Took a while before you confessed your feelings for him."

I balk. "I was scared."

"And that guy who woke me up at the ass crack of dawn this morning was scared too." Easton gives me a look like I'm not getting it.

"We don't know much about him, but you do. Like maybe why he wouldn't wait around..." Calista puts her hand on my arm. She's being the gentlest with me. Always has been.

I shrug. "Probably so he wouldn't have to see me hurt. I did just sit there like a zombie while he told me the story. I'm not even sure I processed it all because I just kept thinking, *he's packed his things, he wants to leave now that he knows.* But I would too, I guess. East is right, I had just gotten out of my grief. And I'm not even sure I *could* continue things with him. Will I always remember that he was there the night Sawyer died? That if one thing had been different, maybe Sawyer would still be alive and I never would've met Van?" A strangled sound erupts from my throat, and I bury my head in my hands. "Why me?"

Calista slides closer, running her hand down my back.

There's a knock on the door and Lance gets up to answer it. A small pit in my stomach is hopeful it's Van because he turned around in case we can make this work, but it's my parents. Lance steps aside to let them in.

"I really wish you guys would let me listen to my gut," my dad grumbles as he comes inside.

My mom rolls her eyes. He comes into the family room and stares at Easton on the chair, flipping through the channels.

It takes Easton a second to notice, then he hurriedly gets up. "Uncle Liam," he says and joins Lance in the kitchen.

My dad sits in the vacated chair and Calista slides over, making room for my mom on my other side.

"What happened?" My mom grabs my hand.

All the tears from two hours ago after he left reemerge.

"It turns out that Van is in the Coast Guard," Calista says quietly.

"Well, we knew he was in the military." My dad shrugs, looking confused.

"He was there that night," she says.

I wipe at the tears, wondering how they haven't run dry yet.

"That night?" My dad shakes his head, clearly not understanding and probably looking like I did when Van started his story.

"*The* night, babe," my mom says, and my dad's eyes widen in understanding.

"He was the diver." Calista tells them all the details of what happened that night as I told them to her, then explains that Van left.

"Fuck life and its curveballs." My dad leans back in the chair, resting one foot on his other knee.

"Oh boy." My mom runs her hand over mine, but I eventually slide it out from under hers because she's going to rub off a layer of skin. "I see now. Should I call a hit man?"

"Mom!"

"I'm kidding. So you don't want him to die?"

"Of course not!" I say.

"The worst part is that he blames himself. He thinks he's the cause of Sawyer's death," Calista says.

It's the first time I realize that I'm not the only one who doesn't blame Van. I know him well enough to know that he did everything he could. There's no question about that. The question is, can I still see Van the same way I did before I knew? Can I look at him and not associate him with Sawyer?

"I'm sure people in his position do that a lot. Can you imagine a really shitty day at work means people die?" My dad shakes his head.

I don't say anything.

"Brin." My dad waits for me to look at him. When I do, he asks me the question point blank. "Can you still see a future with him?"

"It's weird. At first, when he was telling me the story, I couldn't put it all together. I felt like I must be in a dream or nightmare and I'd wake up at any moment. That it was the small amount of guilt I still had for moving on that was manifesting itself, but then I'd wake up happy in Van's arms." I look around the room. "But it's all true and so tragic and such a weird coincidence."

"I'm not sure I think it's a coincidence. Seems more like fate. I mean, the guy who tried to save your husband's life comes to Lake Starlight four years later and ends up being your roommate. Not only that, but you fall for each other as he slowly pulls the old Brinley out of the cold, hard shell you sheltered yourself in after Sawyer's death." We all stare at Easton as he eats a piece of the chocolate cake. "And where the hell is the other half of this frosting?"

I bite my lip as memories of last night flood me. Last night when we both said we wanted our relationship to be something more.

"Easton is a closet romantic," Calista says in an accusatory fashion.

"Fuck that," he says. "But it makes sense."

"As if it was a movie." Calista nods.

"Look how long it took you and Rylan to get your act together," Easton says.

"At least I share myself with people," she says.

"I share myself with people."

"Your dick. You share your dick."

"Okay, you two." My mom puts up her arms to stop their bickering, but I'm enjoying the distraction.

"Maybe you just need time." My dad leans forward and pats my knee.

"No one said you have to decide today," my mom adds.

"It doesn't matter. He left." I shrug.

My parents look at one another and smile.

"He left for your happiness. Not his," my dad says. "He doesn't feel deserving of you. The man I met was already struggling with that. I'm assuming he's shared things with you that he hasn't with us that might make sense to you?" I open my mouth to respond, and my dad puts up his hand. "I don't want to know unless he tells me himself, but something happened to make him feel that way. This whole thing coming to light couldn't have helped." Another pat on my knee. "But you're not going to get there with all of us here. So." He eyes my cousins, and they scramble toward the door. "We're leaving. Don't rush to a decision, Brinley. Take your time. Don't worry, I'll help track him down if you decide he's what you want."

I stand and hug my parents, feeling safe and loved in their arms.

"Liam, you always say the right things," my mom coos.

My dad has his arm around my mom's shoulders, escorting her out of my apartment. Then his footsteps stop, and he stares at the whiteboard.

"'Must wear panties under pajamas. Shirts worn all the time. No masturbating while the other one is home or could come home.'" He shakes his head. "There are some things fathers aren't meant to see."

"I always knew she was kinky," Easton says, and Calista smacks the back of his head.

After I say goodbye to my family and shut the door, the click of the lock echoes in the small apartment. I toss the chocolate cake in the trash and go into my room, picking up my clothes, unsure what to do with myself.

Out of curiosity, I open Van's bedroom door. Sure enough, it's been stripped of the small number of personal items. I step inside, smelling the mix of his cologne and his natural scent that lingers in the room. I crawl into his bed, smell his pillows, and close my eyes, looking for any type of guidance from the universe.

twenty-nine

VAN

It's been one week since I left Lake Starlight, and every night is still torture. So I'm not surprised when I walk into the commander's office and his first words are, "You look like shit. What about the word vacation did you not understand?"

I salute him and he tells me to be at ease, putting his hand out for me to sit.

I hold up my finger and circle it around my face. "This is because of your great advice to get a life."

"You sounded happy the last time I heard from you." He leans back in his chair and puts his feet up on the corner of his desk, displaying his perfectly polished black shoes.

"If I told you what happened, you'd never believe me. Doesn't matter though. I'm here for my reenlistment papers."

I messaged him two days ago to tell him I was back and looking for him to sign my papers.

"The agreement was eight weeks."

"And that changed."

"What happened?"

I shake my head. "I don't want to talk about it." I lean forward and hand him my papers.

He tosses the packet of papers on his desk. "I'm not signing any papers until you do. It's me or a therapist."

I didn't mind my therapist. He did a helluva good job. Although I still have that feeling of hesitation when I know a call isn't going to be routine. He assured me that's the way it is after something like what I went through.

"The woman. Turns out she's one of the widows."

He stares blankly at me. It's a reminder of how much that night lives within me and probably not anyone else. I'm sure my commander has his own nightmares.

"Four years ago."

His head rocks back. "Ah."

"That's all you have to say?"

"It's crazy but not unthinkable. There's not a huge population up here. It's like a story you hear on the *Today Show* or something when siblings find out they've been living in the same town their whole lives and didn't know it. Or did you ever hear about how a scuba diver found a man's wedding ring after his plane crashed and fell in love with the widow when he went to return it to her?"

"Are you reading romance novels?"

He laughs. "Not likely. So, how did you find out?"

"She told me how her husband died. It was easy to put two and two together. Then she showed me a picture, and I knew it was him." My chest tightens as I remember my moment of realization.

"Did you fall in love with this girl?"

"Fall in love? Sir, it was a matter of weeks."

I stare out his window at the new recruits doing their drills. I remember being so happy my first day. I had reliable lodging, food, and camaraderie—something I hadn't had in years. I wonder if another poor bastard like me is in that group, ready to find his or her family here.

"People have fallen in love in a day," he counters.

"Well, I'm not people."

He drops his feet to the floor and spins his chair to face me directly. "Do you want to know what I think?"

"No."

"Too bad. You're scared. Ever since I had you in basic, I've felt this drive to guide you. I've read your file. I know you have no family. Hell, you wrote down a fake number and name for your emergency contact."

I swallow deeply. "So what? I'm not the first seaman who had a shitty childhood."

"No, you're not. But you're the one I took a vested interest in. You always went above and beyond, and the more praise I gave you, the harder you worked. You've been a model seaman and a mentor to many. My problem is you don't see that. All you still see is whatever you were told when you were younger. And I've tried to rip that out of you." He leans back. "I made you go on this leave because eventually, years from now, when you do retire from service, you're going to wonder where the hell your life went and what you have to offer the world if you're not diving into dangerous waters to save someone. I've seen it time and time again."

"I don't think I'm the dumbass my mom's husband told me I was. But saving people... no one prepares you for the high of adrenaline when you bring someone to the helicopter alive. When you see their family rush to them and hug them, crying in happiness that they're alive. And to know you're responsible for that. It's an incredible feeling."

He nods. "It is. I don't disagree, but if you get pulled out of that water, who's running to the person who saved you, thankful you're alive? I mean, besides me." He raises both eyebrows. "This is why I've been so hard on you. Your first four years, you were exactly how you should be. Cocky, arrogant, felt you could save an elephant from drowning in the dead of winter, but these past four years, you're chasing a ghost."

"I'm not." My voice is hard.

"What happened that night isn't your fault. It was three drunk and high guys who panicked when their boat caught on fire. You did what you could, but it was out of your control. It was just a bad night, that's all. Unfortunately, they happen."

"Tell that to her," I say. The look in Brinley's eyes when she told me about the knock on her door will haunt me forever. "Tell that to the young bride who lost her husband. Lost her future. Lost her faith in what life has to offer. Tell her it was just a *bad night*." I hear my voice rising and I know he won't allow me to get away with it for long.

"That answers my first question."

My forehead wrinkles. "What?"

"You do love her."

"Like I said, it's only been weeks. Besides, now that she's found out the truth, she'll never look at me and not blame me for her life changing four years ago."

He stares at me for a long time, then picks up the packet of papers and tosses them at me. "Go ahead and sign them. I can see there's no talking to you about this."

"Finally." I grab his pen and sign all the papers and initial where I need to, then shove them back his way.

"I'll sign it as a witness and file it." I stand and he holds up his hand to stop me from leaving. "It's amazing, isn't it? How you thought life gave you a gift those weeks while you were away, only for it to take the gift back. You've known your entire life that life isn't fair, and maybe she didn't know that until the death of her husband. That doesn't mean it's your fault. It's just life. A twisting and turning road with obstacles, roadblocks, and cliffs. Everyone has a path to navigate. Some get an easy one and others a hard one. Don't you think you've tortured yourself enough? Maybe it's your turn for happiness. God knows you've paid it forward enough with all your saves."

"Do you believe in soul mates, Commander?"

"I believe my wife came into my life when I needed her the most."

I sense he has his own story, and that's why he's always been on my ass.

"She was mine," I say. "In the deepest part of my heart, I know that's the truth. She was my one."

"Then it's a shame you won't fight for her like you fight for all those strangers in the water."

I open my mouth but can't find any words. "Let me know when to report." I salute him.

"You may go."

I walk out the door, shutting it behind me.

His words are haunting, but I know I'm doing the right thing. It would be impossible for her to be happy with the man who caused her husband's death.

BRINLEY

It's been ten days without Van. I've gone over a million scenarios of how we can make this work, but all I see is the pain on his face when he said he'd lost no one until that night. I could clearly see how much that one night haunts him. He worries about me, but I'm a reminder of that loss for him too.

I grab a box and pack up the pictures of Sawyer, going through my drawers and putting away any reminder of him. It's time I move on. It's time I find my future, and it's not going to be in memories of Sawyer.

I realize that every night, I think about Van more. Missing Van more. Yearning for Van more. My sketchbook sits on the floor, and I pick it up, sitting on my bed and flipping through the pages. How did someone who only knew me for a few short weeks know exactly what I needed? How was he able to slowly and gently ease me out of my grief to find myself again?

I tear out the sketch of him naked on my couch and shove it in my drawer. After I'm done packing up my old life, I seal the box with tape and push it to the back of my closet—out of sight but there if I ever want to go through it. Then I grab my purse and sketchbook and head down to my SUV. I stop at the storage locker with all our furniture from the house in it, all of Sawyer's clothes. Then I call the Salvation Army and tell them I have a locker filled with things to donate and schedule a pickup time. Next, I message Lance and Easton and ask if they'd be willing to meet the Salvation Army here whenever they want to schedule the pickup. They both answer yes. Then I message just Lance and tell him I need a plane, and he responds immediately, telling me he'll take care of it.

I leave the storage locker, drive over to Bailey Timber, and park next to my mom's car, heaving out a long sigh when I do.

"Here goes nothing," I murmur.

My heart hammers the entire elevator ride and the walk to my mom's office as if I'm on death row.

Will she be mad? Will she cry? I have no idea what her reaction will be. I was her replacement and now she'll have to start over with someone else.

Her secretary isn't there, so I knock on her door.

"Come in," Mom says.

She's sitting in her desk chair, her reading glasses on, looking over what seems to be a contract.

"Hey, Mom," I say.

She looks up and drops everything, including her glasses. She probably thought I'd never come out of my apartment.

"Look at you," she says, sliding her chair out from the desk and standing to walk toward me. She hugs me hard. "It's so good to see you. You look very put together. Come, let's talk." She leads me to the couch.

"I was cleaning out the storage locker. I'm flying to

Kodiak after this. I want to get a copy of the report. I want to heal and put this behind me. Then I want to find Van."

She pats my knee. "I'm so proud of you. This isn't the easiest decision."

"I love him, Mom. And I have no idea if he'll want to be with me, but I don't want to spend the rest of my life wondering if there's a chance for us."

"Do you want company?"

I shake my head. "But there's something else."

She waits patiently. Here goes nothing.

"When Van was here, and we got closer, he kind of pushed me to do something I've wanted to do for a long time."

"Yeah?"

I dig into my oversized purse and pull out the sketchbook. I hand it to her, and she rests it in her lap. She glances at me and lifts the cover. She doesn't say anything but flips through each page, pausing on some longer than others. Then she hands it back to me and we sit in silence.

"Mom?"

She nods and it's then I notice the tears she's trying to swallow back. "That seals it. You're your dad. I'm not sure what you got from me."

"No, Mom." I wrap my arm around her shoulders. "Don't cry. I look like you."

She offers me a soft smile as her hand runs down her cheek. "I always want you to do what you love. God knows I didn't at first, but I found my love here. I always knew this wasn't for you, but I wanted us to do it together like girl bosses."

I smile and kiss her cheek. "Bring another girl from the family in."

"I hope someone wants to. I'm getting tired." She

stands. "But you have somewhere to be, so go. Do you already have a plane ticket?"

"I have Lance."

She shakes her head. "Thank goodness for the Whitmores, huh?"

I leave my mom and feel a weight come off my shoulders as I leave the building. I'm not sure how I'll support myself financially, but it's time to put all the things I love first.

It feels as though it takes forever for me to get to the airport, though thankfully, the Whitmore private plane is all ready to take me to Kodiak. Doubts fill me during the nearly three-hour flight as I wonder how we'll make the long distance work. But I have to get him back first.

The plane lands, I rent a car, and I drive to the base. I'm allowed a visitor pass, and the guard gives me a map and tells me where I should go. I nod as if I got it, but the map seems turned around and why can't I have GPS?

I reach a dead end and pull the map out again, wondering what I did wrong. A knock on the window startles me, and I look to my left to see an older man in blue slacks and a button-down with a jacket. He has a lot of pins on his left side, which must mean he's important.

"Hi, sir," I say, rolling down the window. "I'm lost."

He laughs. "I figured. Where can I direct you?"

"The records department. I'm trying to get a report from an incident a few years ago. There was an accident."

He rocks back on his heels. "When did it happen?"

"Roughly four years. It was my husband, and I have proof I was his wife."

"It's you," he says.

I frown. "Excuse me?"

"Brinley Kelly?"

My eyebrows shoot up. "How do you know that?"

"Let's say we both care about a certain guy." He points at the empty seat beside me. "May I?"

"Um, sure." I clear off the seat and toss everything in the back. "Are you going to show me to the records department?"

"I'm not sure you'll get the report even if you do find your way there. Besides, it's not going to tell you what you really want to know. How about you let an old man treat you to a coffee?"

I'm so confused, but I decide to go with it. "Okay."

"We have to go off base."

"All right, just point the way."

He gives me directions, and we end up at a little café just outside of the base. We grab our coffees—he insists on paying—then we sit down.

"So, you know Van?" I ask.

He nods. "Since he was eighteen. First off, on behalf of myself and the guard, we are very sorry for your loss." Sincerity rings through his words.

"Thank you."

"It's a shame that this situation is making life even harder on the both of you."

"Have you seen him?" I ask because I have to know how he is.

He nods. "He's probably how you'd expect."

"I'm not sure..."

"He's down, depressed, but stubborn as hell."

I can't fight my smile.

"What do you want to know about the accident?" he asks and sips his coffee.

I shrug. "I'm not sure. Van told me what happened, and I know he was there, but I thought it was four years ago...

maybe he might be remembering it a certain way through his own lens. Maybe there's a way I can convince him it wasn't his fault, and maybe we can... maybe there's a chance for us."

He shakes his head. "Unfortunately, you'll never convince Van he wasn't at fault. That's what we're trained to do, save lives. No matter what happens out there, if someone dies, we'll always take the responsibility."

"Oh," I say as my stomach sinks. There goes my only idea to get him back.

"But it wasn't his fault. It was just a bad situation. Things go wrong all the time. It's amazing how many people we're able to save in situations like that, but sometimes you just can't. It's a hard truth."

"I'm sure."

"I'm the reason Van went to Lake Starlight. Not directly, but that he took leave. I forced him to before I would allow him to reenlist. He was never the same after that accident, and he was so hell-bent on saving as many people as he could afterward. And then he found you, and I heard it in his voice when he called to check in. The man who came into my office a few days ago was a hollow man. A hurt man. I'm not sure anyone can let him see what could be except you."

"Me?" I sip my coffee.

"You're the one who bears the loss of your husband. I thought I could convince him to go after you and fight for you, but I don't think he will until you give him the opening. He needs to feel forgiveness from you. To know that you don't see a monster when you look at him."

I blow out a breath. I could never see a monster when I look at Van.

"I assume that's what you want? You did come all the

way down here, didn't you?" He finishes his coffee and puts down the empty mug. Then he pulls out his phone and texts someone, shoves his phone in his pocket, and walks over to the cashier. She hands him a piece of paper and pen.

Did he just call Van?

He returns, scribbling something down, and pushes the paper toward me. "This is his address. You do what you feel is right."

He sits with me for another ten minutes until a woman pulls up in a minivan and honks.

"That's my ride. Now put that address in your GPS, so you don't get lost this time." He winks and walks away.

"Thank you," I call.

"I'd do about anything for that kid. He really is who you think he is. Life just hasn't been kind to him. It's easy to beat yourself up when that happens." He waves and walks out.

A kid peeks his head out the van window and the commander kisses him. Then he slides into the passenger seat, leans over, and kisses his wife.

I stand and grab the address. *I'm coming for you, Van Adler, whether you're ready for me or not.*

BRINLEY

I arrive at a small cabin on the water and park in the driveway. My gut twists when I see Van's truck because it means he's home, and this will all come to a head—for better or worse.

I ring the doorbell, but no one answers. I look through the little window on the side of the front door and don't see any movement, so I walk along the side of the house, where I hear the distinct sound of an axe hitting wood.

There he is, wearing a skintight shirt that's supposed to keep the heat in, with AirPods in his ears, chopping wood. It's like outdoorsman porn, I swear. He couldn't have been sitting on his couch drinking a beer. Instead he has to be doing the most mouthwatering task, showing me exactly what I'll be missing if he continues to be hardheaded.

He must sense me because he looks over his shoulder and then turns back to his wood, slamming the axe down before turning back to face me. I lift my hand and wave like an idiot. I don't know why. He removes his AirPods from his ears and slowly walks over to me, trepidation about what my visit means in his stride.

"Hey," he says. "What are you doing here?"

"You lied to me."

His eyes widen.

"You told me you'd catch me." I repeat his words that day in his truck when we first had sex. "Actually, you promised. Then you just left. I didn't even get to say anything. So, I'm here for some answers."

He opens his mouth, closes it, and opens it again. "I told you already. It's pretty clear."

"Your job is risky, and I'm pretty sure you knew that when you signed up for it."

"Brinley." He shakes his head.

I put up my hand. "You don't get to decide our fate alone. I get a say too. And I'm ready to move on with my life. I want a life with you. I want to wake up with you next to me. Fall asleep on your chest. I want you to plan dates that push me out of my element. Mostly, I just want you in my life, and I'm willing to take you however I can have you."

He walks to me, but I put my hand on his chest.

"But not if you're broken. Not if every time you look at me, you see your own failures. I can't let you live like that." Tears prick my eyes.

"Brin," he says my name with desperation.

"You're an incredible man, and any woman would be lucky to have you. I desperately want to be her, but that's up to you." I run my hand over his heart. "You gave me my life back and I want to give you yours, but I can't force you. I put all my stuff with Sawyer away, donated all of it except for a small box. I told my mom I didn't want to take over Bailey Timber, that I want to draw. I have no idea how I'll support myself, but at least I'll love what I do."

"I signed the papers. I reenlisted," he admits, looking forlorn.

"Being together doesn't mean we have to be in the same town. You're worth trying long distance for. That's not a deal breaker for me unless it is for you. So, I'm going to leave here, but I'm leaving the door open. Please only step through it if you're one hundred percent in this and you forgive yourself for what happened that night. I already have, though there was nothing to forgive in the first place." I rise on my tiptoes and place a kiss on his lips. "Goodbye, Van."

I turn and walk away back to my rental car. He doesn't come from behind the house, and I start the car. I wait, hoping he'll come, but he never does. I thought he might need more time, and I'm prepared to wait. So I drive back to the airport, with faith that the man I fell in love with will come to his senses.

A WEEK LATER, I'm at Lucky's with Easton and Lance. Lance is talking about how he's finally decided to buy a condo in New York. Although he'll come to visit a lot, we won't be seeing him nearly as much as we're used to. Then again, when Easton is in season, we don't see him very much either.

"Are you going to look up Kenzie?" I ask.

Lance shakes his head. "That's over. She's getting married, right?"

Easton remains quiet, but I don't think it's because he still has feelings for Kenzie. I think he just feels uncomfortable talking about how it all went down between the three of them.

"Yeah, I think next year, maybe?"

I haven't heard from her except for an "I'm so sorry" text when she saw on BuzzWheel that Van had left town. She didn't even call to see why he'd left or how I was doing, but that's been our friendship since she moved to New York. She moves in different circles now.

"Enough about that. So still no word from Van, huh?" Easton asks.

I shake my head. "I'm still holding out faith. It's not like there's a time limit. I just want him to heal."

"Man, I never thought I'd see the day when you'd have all your shit together." I pick up a pretzel and throw it at Lance. He dodges and says, "But it's really nice to see."

"I signed up for a few art classes and my dad's working with me now, although he's more of a freestyler. He asked if I wanted to take over Smokin' Guns when the time came, said that I could work under him and learn to tattoo."

Both of them look at one another and back to me. "Really?" they say in unison.

I nod because I'm really thinking about it. I think I might actually enjoy it. Once I know what the heck I'm doing.

"I feel like I'm sitting with the teenage version of you," Lance says with a smile.

"Me too." I shake my head and tip back my beer.

The door to the bar opens, and a cold breeze flows through the space. Goose bumps rise on my arms. The silence that blankets the room alerts me that something is up, so I turn to see what.

Van stands there surveying the room until his gaze lands on me.

"You're here?" I ask.

He smirks and nods. "Brinley, I always thought of

myself as a loner, definitely never thought I'd be husband material, much less a dad. But ever since you stepped into my life, I've changed. All I want to do is make you happy. Your smile is like being struck by Cupid every damn time. I fall more in love with you than the minute before. I wouldn't even think it was possible. I was a fool for running away, for leaving you, lost in my own shit. But it will never happen again, I promise you. If you give me a second chance, I'll catch you and never let you go."

I grin at him and stand. "What took you so long?"

"I had to make sure I had everything in order."

I narrow my eyes. "What's that mean?"

Nate comes over and hands Van some keys. "Take care of her, okay?"

He shakes Nate's hand. "You have my word."

"What am I missing?" I look between them.

Nate pats Van on the back. "Everyone, meet the new owner, Van Adler. I'm retiring from the bar business and I'm gonna go start a life with my favorite person."

Everyone stands and approaches Nate, giving him their congratulations and asking for details.

Van guides me away from the masses for some privacy.

"I thought you reenlisted?" I ask.

"Turns out my commander never turned in the paperwork. He said he took this young woman out for coffee and figured I'd be changing my mind." He smiles at me.

"He's a really nice guy."

Van nods. "The best mentor ever. But I was hoping you could help me with one part of my relocation back to Lake Starlight?"

"Anything."

"You don't happen to know of a place I could rent, do you?" He smirks, and I bite my lip.

"Funny you should ask. I just put an ad in the paper and I put up a sign looking for a roommate." I point at the bulletin board with a variety of business cards pinned to it.

He walks over to the board as another guy rips my number off the bottom of my flyer. Van yanks the flyer off the board and plucks my number from the guy's fingers. The guy's eyebrows furrow.

"The position has been filled," Van says, then turns to me. "If you'll have me?"

"Who else is going to make me dinner every night?"

I laugh and he steps closer, brushing my hair behind my ear, and we stare into each other's eyes.

"Thank you for saving me," I whisper.

"Hell, you saved me." He dips his head, kissing me as if he's been dreaming of this moment since we've been apart.

Maybe he has because God knows I have been.

One Year Later...

Van lies on the table in front of me, shirtless of course. You'd think now that he's no longer in the Coast Guard, he'd lose his shape, but the man works out all the time. Can I really complain? No.

The stencil is on his skin already and I move forward to do the first ink spot but pull back. "I'm nervous." I set down the tattoo machine and shake out my hands.

"It's natural to be nervous, but honey, I would never set you up to fail. You're ready for this." My dad slides his chair next to mine.

I've been working under him for the past year while attending art classes. My dad and his employees have even tattooed some of my designs on other people, but this is my first time actually tattooing my own design on a person—who also happens to be the man I love.

"Hey, I'm good. I want to be your first." Van takes my hands.

"It won't be the worst one on his body. Look at all his other tattoos," my dad says.

I sigh and stare at him to stop. I know he secretly loves Van but refuses to admit it. Now that their businesses are neighbors, they run into one another a lot.

"Okay, and you're sure about the design? Last chance."

Van hooks his finger under my chin. "I love it not only because you drew it but because of what it represents. The thought you put into it is amazing." He kisses me. "Now let's get on with this."

I start the tattoo machine again, take a deep breath, and work on the outline first. Van doesn't react even though I've seen people get them on their ribs, and it hurts like hell. My dad points out things when I need them and tells me I'm doing great. He lowers his reading glasses to inspect the art better and smiles at me.

Van's eyes close for a while as I get in the groove.

"Hear you two are heading to New York City in a few days?" my dad says.

"Yeah," I say.

"Will you see Kenzie?"

"Doubtful, you know she's getting married, right?" I shake my head but don't take my eyes off Van's skin.

"I can't believe it's not Easton and Lance, truthfully. I thought those three would just agree to cohabitate together. Brother husbands or something."

"Dad!"

"That poor girl was a tug-of-war between them." He grabs the colors I need since I'm almost finished with the outline. I begged my dad to do the shading, not completely confident in my skills, but he refused.

"Actually, she played them at times too. All three of them are responsible for how it all went down." I finish the outline and show it to Van. "You like?"

"I love." He lies back down.

"Well, I think I speak for everyone in town when I say that we're happy she's marrying someone else." My dad sits back down, fiddling with his phone. "Reminds me of your uncle Kingston, Stella, and Owen back in the day."

I nod, remembering the stories I heard over the years. "You okay?" I ask Van for the millionth time.

"Stop asking me. Your hands are on me. I'm perfect."

"Hey now, no hard-ons while we work on you," Moose says from the station across from me.

"I'm her boyfriend," Van argues.

I love the way he holds his own with them. They can be a bit of a tough crowd in here.

"No talk about hard-ons and my daughter." Dad ends the conversation there.

The tattoo takes four hours total, but as I wipe it for the last time, I'm pretty happy with how I did. The colors really pop. I help Van sit up and walk with him over to the standing mirror. He stares at the tattoo for a long time.

The anchor is prominent to symbolize his past life, but also his strength and stability. The rose across the center signifies his passion and love. No one loves as fiercely as Van. And the small butterflies flying out from the anchor represent new beginnings.

"It's beautiful, babe," he says before taking my lips with his.

"You two are gonna have to be careful in bed for a bit," Moose says.

I roll my eyes, but then my dad's there with his phone, wedging himself between us and snapping a photo.

"Oh yeah, I need my photo too." I grab my phone and snap a photo of Van's newest addition to his tattoo collection, proud of the work I did at covering up his scar. It feels good to cover something that only brought bad memories with what I hope only brings him happy ones now.

"Every time I look at it, I'll always think of you." Van kisses me again.

"Let's get it covered."

He lies back on the table, and I put the ointment and plastic wrap on it. When we're finishing up, the door to the shop opens and my mom walks in with a big chocolate cake. Easton and Lance are with her, along with a good portion of my huge family.

"Congratulations!" My mom sets the cake on the counter where people pay in the lobby area and slides through the half door. "My baby, a tattoo artist," she says, shaking her head.

Everyone congratulates me, and we chat and eat cake for a while. Halfway through the party, I see Van talking to my uncles and cousin. They're laughing, having a great time, and warmth spreads through my chest. He's one of us now, and hopefully he'll never feel alone in this world again. The Baileys have taken him in as one of our own.

Later on, we take the rest of the chocolate cake home, but this time I smear the icing up and down his cock, bringing him to the edge with my mouth as his hands grip my hair. Life doesn't get any better than this. Turns out you can have your dessert and eat it too.

FOUR DAYS LATER...

. . .

I'M SITTING in the taxi in New York on our way to meet Lance. Van's hand is on my thigh, and he keeps running circles with his fingers and then running his palm up and down. I finally put my hand on his to stop him.

He looks at me quizzically and I tilt my head. Our nonverbal way of saying "What" and "You know what."

I can't wait until the damn tattoo is healed so we can go crazy again. We've had to be creative with our positions and keep things pretty tame.

We stop at a light outside a church where a bride and groom are walking out as people blow bubbles toward them. They look so happy and I silently wish them happiness for the rest of their lives together.

He leans over. "Do you want all that when we get married?"

"I don't know. I had it once, but I can't imagine my family not being there either and there's so many of us it's hard to travel."

He nods. "Yeah, that's true. But we could just have a small wedding on the grounds of the cabin."

I took Van to my great-grandma's cabin, and he fell in love with it. I had to explain to him that it's not really ours and I think he was disappointed. Calista wants it passed to each cousin. In fact, she told me I have to figure out who the next person is to get it now that I've found love. Seems she's really taking on Great-Grandma Dori's mission as her own with our generation.

"Maybe we could ask," he says.

I nod and hold up my left hand. "We're missing a key item."

"Don't you worry about that." I look at him long and hard because he's got something up his sleeve. I can tell.

I wave myself with my hand. "It's getting hot in here."

I can't stand it when taxi drivers don't use the air conditioning. I get that it's unusually hot right now for New York, but come on, my makeup is dripping down my face.

"We were supposed to be there like fifteen minutes ago," I say.

Van shrugs. I wonder how he can be so high-strung sometimes but mellow other times.

We sit in traffic for another fifteen minutes when my phone vibrates in the small purse I have on my lap.

> Lance: Stop fucking and get your ass to the restaurant.

A LAUGH BUBBLES out of me, and I show Van the screen of my phone.

"I wish," he mumbles.

> Me: We've been in traffic forrreevvveerrr. The place you chose better have air conditioning.

> Lance: I picked a place not that far from your hotel, why didn't you walk?

> Me: Hello, did you not feel the heat when you walked out of your condo this morning? It's like one hundred degrees.

> Lance: It's your Alaskan blood.

Lance: I ran into someone, so I have a nice
surprise for you.

MY PHONE DROPS in my lap, and I whip my head in the direction of Van. He rears back. "What?"

"I don't know anyone but Lance and Kenzie in New York." I pick up my phone and show him the text.

"You think it's her?" he asks.

"I think I'm going to kill someone if it is. She's supposed to be getting married."

He rests his hand on my leg again and squeezes. "Remember, it's not your life."

I say nothing but inhale a deep breath as if meditating will help me. Van doesn't know everything that went down with Kenzie, Lance, and Easton. I had high hopes she'd get married and it would all just go away.

Finally, the taxi pulls up to the curb, and I open the door, eager to feel a breeze or something while Van pays the driver.

Sure enough, the minute I open up the door to the fancy restaurant Lance picked for lunch, a screech echoes throughout the room and Kenzie throws herself at me, throwing her arms around my neck, plastering herself to me.

I give Lance my best death stare, but he only shrugs. Sometimes I hate having guy best friends. They really don't understand some shit the way women do.

"Oh my god!" Kenzie draws back and looks me up and down. "You look gorgeous, and this must be Van." She puts her hand out, and Van accepts it.

"Nice to meet you."

"The pleasure is all mine. I was supposed to meet my fiancé here, so imagine my surprise when he canceled, and I bumped right into Lance."

"What a coincidence," I say dryly.

She walks us over to the table and we all say hello. I pinch Lance in the back of the arm, and he retracts, giving me an evil glare. He's the one who brought her. I know I'm just upset because seeing her in person reminds me of the old Kenzie—the small-town girl who changed when she moved here. The girl I'm no longer that close to.

We all sit, and I'm barely able to glance at the menu before she starts talking again. Van puts his hand on my leg, and I think it's to calm me, but even his touch isn't working.

"So, we've had all these problems with the press lately. Somehow they keep figuring out the details of our wedding. My fiancé's father is Wendell Asbury." She waits for us to react, but we don't. We all already knew she was engaged to the real estate tycoon's son. She waves her hand when we stare blankly. "Anyway, Lance gave me a great suggestion when we were chatting—we should have the wedding in Lake Starlight. Remember when we'd dream about having double weddings on the lake?"

I'm so surprised I don't say anything for a beat. When I recover, I say, "You're going to get married on the lake?"

"The press will never think we'd have it all the way up in Alaska. It's perfect." She puts her hand on top of Lance's, and I stare at it, wishing I had the powers to laser it off.

Lance gently slides his hand out from under hers and when our eyes meet, mine blazing, he shrugs again. Oh, we're gonna have words.

I deserve an Emmy for my performance during lunch and after we say goodbye outside the restaurant, Lance and

Kenzie decide to share a taxi uptown, and I'm about ready to explode.

"Let's go up to the top of the Empire State Building. I've never been." Van points to where we can see it sticking up between some lower buildings.

My mouth drops open. Does he not notice that now might not be the time? "Seriously?"

"What else do we have to do now? Don't let that ruin our day."

He kind of has a point. We can still have a fun day in New York City. So, we walk in that direction. He pays for our tickets, and we wait in line for the elevator.

"I can't believe Lance. I told him when he moved here to keep his distance from her. Oh god, have they been having an affair?" I ask out loud, but Van doesn't chime in.

He starts talking to the people next to us who are from Florida. He's asking for places to visit there and when he says he's from Alaska, he gets the same questions you always get as an Alaskan which mostly relate to people's assumptions of what it's like to live there. Like, do moose just walk next to our cars on the highway and is it either always dark or always light, never in between?

I'm still muttering to myself about Lance and how he's putting himself in a bad situation when the elevator reaches the top.

Van takes my hand and leads me out to the observation deck. "It's beautiful," he says. "Let me take a picture of you." He positions me with the skyline behind me. "Smile."

I smile and he takes the picture.

I look back out at the view, silently contemplating until I say, "Van, you're gonna have to talk to him." It's then I notice he's not standing next to me. I look to my right and my left, but there are just strangers staring at me... smiling. Creepy.

"Brin!" Van says my name, and I spin around then look down to see him on bended knee. He has a box open with a sparkling diamond ring nestled inside.

"Oh my god," I say, wanting to bend down to his level, but he slides closer and takes my left ring finger.

"This past year has been the best of my entire life and I selfishly want you by my side for as many more years as I have on this earth. Will you marry me?"

A crowd is forming, and people are oohing and aahing.

"Of course!" My tears spill over, and he slides the ring onto my finger, snapping the box shut and stuffing it in his pants before standing. Then he presses his lips to mine.

"I love you," he whispers and kisses me again.

"I love you." I hug him and rest my head on his chest.

The best place on earth is in his arms and I will never take one second of our time together for granted. The universe gifted me with another great love, and I have no plans to squander this gift.

Can't get enough of Brinley and Van's story?
We've written a special BONUS SCENE for you!

CLICK HERE

*Please note by downloading the Bonus Scene you are agreeing to join our newsletter if you're not already a subscribed member.

Is Lance's wedding venue suggestion to Kenzie as innocent as he claims? Find out in the next Lake Starlight book, The Trouble with Runaway Brides!

CLICK HERE

Rayne's been dying to write a young widow story for a while, and as much as we all wish things were perfect in Lake Starlight, that would make for some pretty boring books. So, we picked Brinley to be our young widow who lost her husband as a newlywed.

This story went a lot of places, at first our hero was going to be the complete opposite of Liam—a conservative guy who wore a suite to work, but then we thought it would be more fun to see Liam's reaction when his daughter wanted to date someone who outwardly looked a lot like him. We even played with the idea of making Van a tattoo artist working under Liam but as much as some of you might not have minded that, it felt too much like we were writing Liam and Savannah's story all over again.

As you know, we like to stack on trope on top of trope and the roommate trope was decided on at the end of Calista and Rylan's book. A light bulb just went off and that's why they wouldn't be able to get away from another. Forced proximity for the win!

We will say, keeping the secret about how Sawyer died, and that Van was the diver was tricky for us. We had to do it in a way that Van didn't KNOW he held the secret. We wonder how many of you guessed it?

Lake Starlight is our happy place and it's so awesome writing stories in this world and bringing in cameos of other family members!

As always, we have a lot of people to thank for getting this book into your hands...

Nina and the entire Valentine PR team.
Cassie from Joy Editing for line edits.
Ellie from My Brother's Editor for line edits.
Rosa from My Brother's Editor for proofreading.
Hang Le for the cover and branding for the entire series.
Wander Aguiar for his awesome job of photographing our muses for Brinley and Van.
Bloggers who consistently carve out time to read, review and/or promote us.
Piper Rayne Unicorns who are always so supportive and tell all their friends that they should be reading our stories.
Readers – There are so many options out there and we're both honored and grateful that you took some of your precious time to send inside a world of our creation. We hope we didn't let you down.

You already know who's going to get the letter from Grandma Dori in the next book. Yep, our billionaire heir, Lance Whitmore, Brooklyn and Wyatt's son! Can't wait—we love a runaway bride!

xo,
Piper & Rayne

about piper & rayne

Piper Rayne is a USA Today Bestselling Author duo who write "heartwarming humor with a side of sizzle" about families, whether that be blood or found. They both have e-readers full of one-clickable books, they're married to husbands who drive them to drink, and they're both chauffeurs to their kids. Most of all, they love hot heroes and quirky heroines who make them laugh, and they hope you do, too!

My Vegas Groom

A Greene Family Summer Bash

My Sister's Flirty Friend

My Unexpected Surprise

My Famous Frenemy

A Greene Family Vacation

My Scorned Best Friend

My Fake Fiancé

My Brother's Forbidden Friend

A Greene Family Christmas

The Modern Love World

Charmed by the Bartender

Hooked by the Boxer

Mad about the Banker

The Single Dads Club

Real Deal

Dirty Talker

Sexy Beast

Hollywood Hearts

Mister Mom

Animal Attraction

Domestic Bliss

Bedroom Games

Cold as Ice

On Thin Ice

Break the Ice

Box Set

Charity Case

Manic Monday

Afternoon Delight

Happy Hour

Blue Collar Brothers

Flirting with Fire

Crushing on the Cop

Engaged to the EMT

White Collar Brothers

Sexy Filthy Boss

Dirty Flirty Enemy

Wild Steamy Hook-up

The Rooftop Crew

My Bestie's Ex

A Royal Mistake

The Rival Roomies

Our Star-Crossed Kiss

The Do-Over

A Co-Workers Crush

Hockey Hotties

My Lucky #13

The Trouble with #9

Faking it with #41

Sneaking around with #34

Second Shot with #76

Offside with #55

Kingsmen Football Stars

You Had Your Chance, Lee Burrows

You Can't Kiss the Nanny, Brady Banks

Over My Brother's Dead Body, Chase Andrews

Chicago Grizzlies

Something like Hate

Something like Lust

Something like Love

Standalones

Single and Ready to Jingle

Claus & Effect